I0546009

These titles are available from the same author …

Pierced, Padlocked and Tamed
Missy in Breast Bondage
Victoria's Ordeal
Victoria's Confinement
Maggie's Enslavement
Maggie's Bondage Training
Maggie Becomes the Fixed Filly

and . . .

Pussy: A Guide for Men

Look for them in e-book and paperback formats …

Pierced, Padlocked and Tamed

Lander Moore

ReagePress

Copyright 2014 ReagePress

ISBN 978-1-7326167-0-7

e-mail: ReagePress@gmail.com

Helen was alone, cold and cramped, in a nearly empty loft, with just a few odds and needs of stuff scattered on the floor. No furniture, but a bar on one side of the large room, and a pulley in the ceiling

She was on her knees, naked, with cords of rope binding her legs tightly above her knees; her ankles were bound as were her arms. It seemed to her that yard after yard of rope had been used, to wrap her arms tightly together, behind her back, from her wrists to her elbows… If she could have seen herself, she would have seen her own arms bound in white, like gloves, from wrists to elbows. But all she knew was that her arms ached and ached. She felt her arms and shoulders go numb long ago; now there was only an insistent throb of pain from her shoulders.

The way her arms were tied behind her back made her breasts jut out. Ropes had been crisscrossed over and under her breasts, the rope cutting into her back, then under her left breast, then over her right; over her right breast, under her left and under her arms and across her back. She couldn't decide which hurt more, the throb of her arms and shoulder blades or the sharper cut of the ropes across her back and over and under her breasts. Wide white adhesive tape was crisscrossed over her mouth; she could say nothing, except moan slightly behind the tape.

She had been bound in the morning—she long ago lost track of the time—it must be after noon or

5

perhaps late in the afternoon or even night—she had no way of knowing. All she knew of her world was the pain of the ropes cutting into her and the ache in her arms and shoulders. She felt a throb of pain with every heartbeat and with every breath. When her heart beat, she felt the throb and stab of pain through her pinioned arms and shoulders. When she tried to take a deep breath, the ropes cut deeper into her chest. Breathing was so difficult without making the pain worse; she had to breathe slowly and carefully. If she accidentally took a quick deep breath, pain encircled her chest. She learned quickly to take very careful breaths so she wouldn't make the pain any stronger.

She wore a black leather dog collar and a small padlock locked into her neck. Usually the padlock was at the back of her neck, but it had been moved— the collar had been taken off and turned so the lock was at the front of her neck. At the back was a chrome ring. Rope had been fed through the ring and pulled through the pulley in the ceiling. Helen was made to sit very straight. She could not relax because the ring and the rope would not let her. She could not lie down in any way; the rope held her back straight.

So she stayed, counting her own heartbeats for something to do, counting her own breathing, being careful not to breathe too quickly, to make her chest heave too quickly, for that too made the ropes cut into her more. The ache in her shoulders was constant.

She had first thought that when she was used to the pain in her shoulders and arms—after she got used to it—the pain would somehow lessen and become more bearable. She was surprised when it did not lessen—the pain was constant. A throbbing, pulsating that never lessened. She could never anticipate that it would die down; her bound arms thrust her chest out. But with the ropes across her back and crisscrossed over and under her breasts, she suffered double agonies. If she tried to lessen the pain by arching forward, to lessen the cramps in her shoulders, she only served to tighten the constricting ropes across her chest. If she tried to lessen the ache in her chest by leaning back, the very slight movement backwards made her arms and shoulder blades throb even more.

She was awash with pain, steady uncompromising pain. She drifted with the pain and let it ebb and flow from her chest to her arms, shoulder blades and back, then again, focusing in her arms and chest again.

She learned she was able to focus every few minutes ever so slightly on one part of her body and thus ignore, if she could—ever so much—the pains and throbbings elsewhere. So she lost count of her heartbeats and her own breathing and focused on her bound arms for a time; ignoring the pain—as much as she could ignore it—which was precious little—the pain in her chest and back. Then she was able to focus on the pain in her chest and back—the ropes which cut so deeply into her back and crisscrossed under and over her breasts.

Then the pain in her bound arms and shoulder blades seemed to be ever-so-slightly blocked from her mind—at least momentarily. Then the pain in her arms and back and shoulder blades would creep back and she would have to concentrate on that; ignoring as much as possible as she could, the wracking, the throbbing, pulsating, pounding pains in her chest, the ropes across her chest and across her back.

Thus she spent the day, alternatively concentrating on her own arms and shoulder blades, then on her bound chest, then back to her bound arms and the dull constant throbbing pain in her shoulders.

She lost count of the time, the minutes, the hours. All she knew was the pain the ropes caused her. She did not daydream; did not let her memory wander through her past; she did nothing except concentrate on the ropes, her arms, her shoulders, her chest.

All she knew was the constrictions the ropes caused, the aching, throbbing pain.

She kept her eyes open for a time, then closed her eyes against the pain and the discomfort. She felt somehow better with her eyes closed—it made her job of concentrating on the pain easier. So she knelt, bound and aching, her eyes closed, concentrating on the pain which the yards and yards of rope caused her.

Finally she heard! Steps downstairs. A door slamming. Footsteps on the stairs. Someone coming. Frank? Others? How many? One man? Two? More? She listened carefully. Only one. One person. Frank, coming back alone. She was positive. Frank. Alone.

She watched the door open. It was Frank. Alone. She watched him walk over to her. He stood in front of her.

"Still bein' a bitch today?"

She shook her head. NO.

"You say you won't be bitchy, but that doesn't last long—then you're back to being a real bitch again. We have to work on that—you're not very obedient— yet. There's still a lot of the bitch in you. You keep forgetting…"

She wanted to tell him how badly her arms and shoulders hurt and that she would be good if only he let her up, but with the white tape across her mouth she could only look at him.

He slowly pulled the tape from her mouth.

"Want to get up now?"

"Yes, please. My arms and shoulders hurt so."

He loosened the rope that had held her head up so straight, then began to unwrap the yards of rope that had bound her arms so tightly behind her back. She waited silently, waited for her freedom. Having her arms suddenly free made then ache differently— she knew that it would be some time before the cramps and pain left her arms, because she had been bound so long.

He pulled her to her feet and untied the ropes from her legs then untied the ropes from around her knees.

Free! Free from being on her knees all day. She took a tentative step, then another. She waited for him untie the ropes which had bound her chest too tightly. Yards and yards of white rope lay at her feet. Frank finally got all the rope untied and dropped it onto the pile at her feet. She arched her back. She was naked, but having her freedom meant so much to her that she momentarily forgot her nudity. Then she remembered how cold she had been on the floor, naked and bound.

Frank lit a cigarette and watched her.

She walked across the room toward the mattress on the floor, where her clothes had been left, just before Frank had tied her up that morning. She reached for her shirt to pull on. Her cut-offs? Where had he put her cut-offs? She was so cold she—

—was jerked backwards. Wearing an old shirt, not yet buttoned, Frank had pulled her by her hair. Sparks of white shot through her head. Such a sharp pain, she didn't know what—

"Did I tell you to put that on? Bitch?" He shook her violently by her hair.

"No Frank, but I was—I was so cold—"

He turned her around and held her by her upper arms.

"Did I say you could get dressed? Did you hear me say anything about getting your clothes on?"

"No Frank, I—"

He suddenly turned her sideways and smacked her on her behind. It made her jump and yip with the sudden pain. When he held her by her arms the same pain she had endured all day returned.

"Frank, I—"

"You still don't learn, do you? You do what I want you to do. When I tell you to do it. You don't get dressed without asking. You don't stand without asking. You don't do anything without waiting for me to tell you what to do." He slapped her behind again and she jumped and yipped again and trued to protect her behind with one hand. He pulled her hand away, held both her wrists in one hand and spanked her again.

"Please Frank, oh don't please. I was so cold. I didn't think—no—please—don't—" She winced and twisted away from him as much a she could with him holding her wrists.

"No. Please. PLEASE. Frank—"

He waited until her twisting subsided. She finally stood in front of him without moving. He continued to hold her wrists with his left hand, his right hand cocked to smack her again on her behind.

"You just don't listen Helen. You just don't listen. You don't learn anything from day to day. Eventually I'll make you behave. You really are a bitch, you know it? But you will learn how to behave. Then you'll be proud of how you've changed, But it sure will take a while…" He pulled her back to where the rope hung from the pulley in the ceiling. She began to cringe.

"No, Frank. Please. I'll behave. I'll be good. Don't. Please. Not again. Not some more. Please. I won't be bad. I've been tied all day. Please don't. Not again. Don't."

But she was helpless; he was so strong. Frank pulled her arms behind her and quickly tied her wrists with the rope, with her wrists crossed behind her back. Thank goodness it was a different position. She didn't think she could stand to have her arms bound the same way as they had been all day. The different position—with her wrists crossed—at least wasn't as bad as having her arms bound from the wrists to her elbows, her palms together.

She continued to twist and squirm but he finished quickly.

He stood in front of her and held her by her upper arm.

"I thought you would have learned something by being tied all day by yourself. Don't' you learn anything?"

"Yes Frank, it hurt so bad. I thought I couldn't stand it. Please, I—"

He slapped her on the side of her hip. "That isn't what I meant. Didn't you think at all about how obedient you said you'd be?"

"Yes—Frank—I—"

"You haven't learned much. Let's see how you can learn and behave now. Stand still…"

He left her standing in front of the rope hanging from the pulley, walked across the loft and got a wide leather belt.

Helen began to cringe again as he walked back to her.

"You're not going to spank me with that—are you? Frank? No, not that—"

"No. Not that," he mimicked. "Hold still." He wrapped the belt around her waist and buckled it tightly onto her. He reached down, doing something on the floor. Hunting for something. The rope. The end of the rope. The rope that hung from the pulley. The rope that had kept her upright and sitting so straight on her knees all day. He pulled the end of the rope up and tied it to the belt, just above her navel.

"Stand still." He walked behind her and began doing something. She knew. The rope. The slack began to disappear. He was pulling it tight. Right between her legs. She saw all the slack disappear. She stepped apart—her legs about a foot apart on the floor.

She felt the rope creep up between her legs. Frank stopped, held one part of the rope and stepped in front of her again.

"You've had your legs together all day. Let's see how well you do with your feet apart." He guided the rope down from the belt, across her slit, across her pussy and down, down between her legs. She felt it settle in the cleft between her buttocks. Then she felt the rope tighten. Then more. And more.

"Frank—I—don't. Please." She tried to grab the rope with her bound wrists, but couldn't grab it behind her back."

"Frank, it's tight. Too tight. Don't. Please stop—"

But he didn't stop. The rope seemed to cut her in two. She finally had to stand on her tiptoes to try and keep the rope from cutting into her. The pain was sharp, more intense than the full, throbbing pain in her arms and shoulders—the pain that she had endured all day. This was much more—much more intense. More unbearable than the other pain.

"Frank—it's cutting into me so."

She watched him. He had apparently tied the rope so she was standing on her tiptoes. He walked across the loft and got a can of beer from the refrigerator, popped the top, drank half of it with his back to her, then returned.

He slapped her on her hip again and made her sway and teeter on her tiptoes. The swaying made the rope cut into her differently; each movement ever so slightly caused her different pain. She hoped her wouldn't think to make a game of it—to see how much she could dance on her tiptoes with the rope cutting into her.

"Frank—it's cutting me in two—"

"Where babe? Can you tell me? You know the words." He again slapped her left hip so she did a small dance on her toes.

"It's in me—"

"Where? Again the slap. Again she danced back and forth a few inches on her toes.

"In my—in my slit."

"Try some more words." A slap again, Harder. On her other hip, making her dance, changing the pain slightly inside her.

There was an edge of pain and fear in her voice.

"In my pussy. It's cutting my pussy in two. And my butt."

"Know any other words?" He drained the beer and threw the can toward a corner of the loft, then slapped her harder on her right hip. She again danced on her tiptoes a few inches, as much as the rope would permit.

"In my snatch. In my pussy. And it's cutting my ass in two."

"Feel like screaming?"

"In a minute. Oh, I can't stand it. Please Frank. I'm being cut in two. In my pussy. Oh, please—"

He spread he pussy lips apart with a thumb and index finger. "The rope's inside you. But you won't be cut in two. It just feels like you're being cut in two. Now aren't you sorry for being such a bitch?"

"Yes, Yes. Please Frank. I'm sorry…" she began to thrash around, a much as she could.

"If you scream I'll put the tape over your mouth again. Do you want that?"

"No Frank, but it hurts so bad. Don't please. Let me down."

He stepped back and surveyed her.

"You can stand it for a while. Then maybe you'll behave for the rest of the night."

He stepped in front of her, took her hips in both hands and swung her to each side until she felt her toes leave the floor. Then he let her swing, the rope cutting into her. She did a frantic dance. Trying to stand straight on the floor, on her toes, to keep the rope from biting, from cutting into her, but he had swung her to the sides so much she didn't have much chance to stand straight—she had to tiptoe for a few minutes until the momentum of the swaying died down and she could stand in place. Frank watched her dance with amusement. Then he came back to her.

"I think you'll need the tape in a few minutes." He walked over to where he had left the roll of white athletic tape, came back and taped her mouth closed, with two strips of crisp-crossing tape. She could just mumble and shake her head.

Frank knew that the stress of the rope cutting into her pussy was getting greater—that the pain was building instead of remaining the same; he knew she would begin to moan soon, then cry or perhaps scream. The tape kept her mouth closed and that, somehow, made the pain worse—she would have had an avenue to release the pain if she had been able to scream. The tape kept the pain within her and made it build and build.

Helen began slowly to thrash around, to shake her head; her eyes widened, she began to breathe harder, her nostrils flaring. She thrashed her shoulders back and forth, dancing on the floor with her toes. Frank came to her and pushed her back and forth by shoving her hips.

Her eyes widened even more, her nostrils flared with each breath. Behind her back, she balled her hands into fists, unclenched them, balled them again in an attempt to focus attention on her fists instead of the pain in her pussy and inside her butt.

She tried to dig her fingernails into her palms, hoping that the pain of her fingernails into her palms would distract her from the sharp biting, digging pain in her pussy. But nothing could distract her from the pain she was suffering with the rope imbedded in her pussy, cutting her slit in two, cutting into the crack of her butt.

Frank walked up to her and held her by her hair.

"Should I tie your legs off the floor? I could, you know. I could just double a rope around your ankles and pull them up behind your knees. Then you'd have all your weight on the rope in your pretty little pussy. Would you like that? All I'd have to do is hold you so you didn't fall over and all your weight would be on the rope. Then it *would* feel like you're being cut in two.

"Or—" and he thought of a different method, "All I'd have to do would be to pull the rope so your toes are off the floor. Can you imagine what it would be like have all your weight—*all your weight*—on the rope? Between your legs? All your weight on the rope in your slit?

"Then you would feel like a very, very good little pussy, a *very very* good little pussy. A few minutes a day with the rope so you're off your feet and your weight entirely on the rope in your snatch would make a new woman out of you, I guarantee it, Helen. Think that over..."

She was thinking about it.

That would be hideous.

She didn't think she could bear that. She prayed that Frank wouldn't do that to her. But it would be so simple for him to do it. All he would have to do would be to adjust the rope a little bit more—a little more, pull her up a little more, so that not even a fraction of her weight was on her toes, on the floor. She tried to imagine what that little bit more would mean to the pain in her slit. She hoped and prayed that Frank wouldn't do that to her. She wanted to tell him how good she'd be, but the tape across her mouth prevented her from saying anything. She was *beg*, she would plead with him, she'd do anything, anything if he would only let her down. If he would only let her down so that awful rope wasn't splitting her pussy in two. Her pussy, her snatch—she knew it was being absolutely cut in two. And he didn't care! He seemed to find it amusing. Well, she'd just tell him—No.

That was what got her into trouble in the first place. She *had* been a bitch with him. She was rude and snippy. A chrome-plated bitch. And he showed her who was boss. Tying her so she was naked and on her knees all day—her hands bound—her arms, from her wrists to her elbows, all white with rope so she couldn't move. And now this—just because she wanted to get dressed after he let her down.

She never thought she knew such pain. And she never thought she could stand such pain. But she was! She was surprised at herself. Minute after minute, the stabbing, cutting absolutely wretched agonizing pain. It never got any easier. She had to constantly balance on her toes.

Frank finally came back to her and carefully pulled the tape from her mouth and let her down— she was so relieved. But suddenly he pulled her back again so just her toes were on the floor. The pain slackened, then quickly returned. She squealed with the returning pain.

"How about it? Are you going to be bitchy for the rest of the night?" He held her by the back of her head—by her hair.

"No. Please let me down."

"No what?"

"No I won't be a bitch. Please let me down."

"No *Sir*. No Sir. I won't be a bitch."

She looked at him. "No Sir. I won't be a bitch. Please let me down."

Frank let loose of her hair.

"Your little pussy isn't damaged much. I think you ought to show me it works just fine. I think you need to have it full of something nice and hard to show me that it still works just fine."

"No. Please—I—"

"It's that or your mouth. You'll learn you can't say no to me. Your beautiful pussy or your mouth. Or—" he paused, "or your butt. What other words do you know for that?"

She was suddenly frightened again.

"No Frank. You wouldn't do that in my behind. Not do that to me—"

"Make up your mind. Or you won't be let down. You have three choices. Make up your mind. The longer you wait, the longer you hang here."

What a choice! But she had brought it on herself.

"I can't. Not in my behind. Not in my ass. My pussy is so sore—I—not in my pussy—not now. Frank. Please. Just let me down."

"That leaves one choice—" he said, as he loosened the rope. He left her hands bound—her wrists crossed and bound behind her back. He lowered her to her knees. She closed her eyes. At least anything was preferable to having him in her sore, aching pussy. Her poor little hurting slit. She heard a mechanic *ziiiippp* and opened her eyes just in time to see him unzipping his fly.

She closed her eyes again. She felt his thumb and forefinger at her mouth. He pried her mouth open. She kept her eyes closed. His thing, his erect thing, slid into her mouth. He kept her chin cupped with one hand and held the back of her head with his other hand. He worked and worked and worked. Sometimes slow and steady and sometimes hard and fast, trying to make her gag. And she did gag—time after time. Almost raping her mouth. She kept her eyes tightly closed the entire time, breathing through her nose. He finally came then, spurting his cum, his semen, into her throat. She tried to pull away from him, but he held her head and didn't slip out of her mouth until he was sure she had swallowed. All of him.

"One more thing," he said, before he let her go.

"You have to learn to like it. Not ever try to push away from me." Then he untied her wrists and let her up.

I'll never learn to like it like that, she thought to herself. But she didn't say anything more to him. She staggered over across the loft to a daybed and fell onto it, exhausted.

* * *

Helen always thought she was probably born bitchy. She could remember being cranky and bitchy to her Mother (her father died before she could remember him)and, as she got older, she remembered being bitchy to her sister, Kathy, three years younger. Helen wanted her own way always, and usually got it. When she was a child, she got her way by having tantrums; when she got older, she learned to get her own way by being irritable, aloof and demanding.

She had always lived in southern California; when she was old enough to go to college, she went to U.S.C. She avoided sororities in college and ended up being called the "Ice Queen," because of her bitchiness. She dated occasionally but always found that college boys deferred to her; she seldom slept with any of them—she found them to be—well, just *boys*.

Physically she had the natural attractiveness which had come to be called the "California look," Tall, leggy, with ash blonde hair which fell to the nape of her neck. She had almost a model's stature, especially with her aloofness, which somehow was a physical attribute, but she didn't have quite the natural model's way of walking and she didn't pay enough attention to the secrets of make-up to be a model. But she was attractive, especially in designer jeans, and boots, which emphasized her behind, her legs and her carriage.

She trimmed her pubic hair, just for amusement—

it matched the ash blonde of her hair, but trimmed, it was almost invisible. She liked the look of having almost no pubic hair at all.

She graduated from U.S.C. with a degree in business and found a job with a stock brokerage firm in San Francisco. She didn't want to leave California just for a job—the stock market wasn't quite her specialty, but the job paid well enough. She came to enjoy the hills and the fog and the exotic landscape of San Francisco—the scenes, the foods, the beauty of the "City by the Bay." She discovered, somewhat to her surprise, that most of the men in San Francisco were either gay or married. Most of the men in her stock brokerage firm were gay, some obvious, some not.

She didn't have much luck meeting the type of men she thought she would prefer—but then again— she never knew what kind of men she really liked. The college boys did nothing to, or for, her. The gays were out, even thought many of them were charming and gracious and some knew how to cook and decorate. The rest, or so it appeared to her, were married and she simply didn't want the hassle of dating a married man or trying to be someone's mistress when he had the little wife at home.

So she worked without much enthusiasm, traveled occasionally, and was as bitchy as she had always been. On the weekends, she wore her jeans and boots and sweaters, and sometime despaired of meeting Mr. Right, as the women's magazines called *that special man.*

But she never knew what kind of man was right for her. Certainly not the man, or men, who deferred to her, who were super polite and agreed with her and let her have her way, whenever she had a snit or began to bitch about whatever happened to cross her way.

On a dare once, she and another girl from the firm, a secretary she barely knew, drove across the Bay to a bar which the girls knew was a biker's handout. The two of them knew—or assumed—they would be safe. Certainly they wouldn't be raped just because they went slumming on a Saturday night in a bar on the outskirts of Oakland. They got lost on the way and had to ask directions at a gas station.

Eventually they found the bar: the "Roamin' Eye," a concrete block, non-descript bar, with painted-over windows and twelve motorcycles outside, which they knew were called choppers.

At first Helen was disappointed. There were only about 12 men inside, shooting pool, or watching a TV set high above the bar, tuned to a football game. There were three or four biker "momas," hanging around—the biker girlfriends, but they didn't say anything to Helen and her friend and they didn't say anything to the other women.

Helen and her friend Crissy sat down and ordered beers. Helen became more and more fascinated by the men. They all wore their colors, jeans, heavy boots, t-shirts, levi vests. All the vests had the name of their club:

Los Gatos, which she vaguely remembered from her college Spanish was probably *The Cats* or *The City Cats*. The backs of all their levi vests showed a snarling black panther with the word *Oakland* across the bottom.

All their t-shirts had obscene slogans on the front: *Bikers Give Better Head*; *I'll Eat Pussy*; *Bikers Get Laid More* and others. Or they had the Harley-Davidson emblem, the spread-winged eagle, and a variety of riding slogans: *Ride to Live, Live to Ride*; *God Rides a Harley*; *Fuck Helmet Laws*; *Sworn to Fun, Loyal to None* and others. Two or three of the biker women wore tank-tops and they also had obscene sayings: *I'm in Heat*; *I'm an Easy Rider*; *Screw Housework* and one that Helen smiled at: *My Body's an Outlaw—It's Wanted All Over Town*.

She was amazed at the variety of obscene sayings they wore and all seemed to enjoy.

In the front of the men's vests were their names—and again Helen was amazed at the variety of outlandish names or nicknames they had: *Charger Charley*, *Little Jesus*; *Buzzard*; *Frenchy*; *Muther*; *Freddy Fudpucker*; *Magoo*; *The Animal*—each more outrageous than the last. Most of the men wore an earring in one ear; most looked like they hadn't shaved in weeks; a few smelled. Most were routinely obscene—each sentence seemed to include *motherfucker*.

Helen watched them, discreetly, while nursing a couple of beers. They seemed to treat their "momas," with a casual disregard for femininity. They seemed to expect that their women were always hot—always in heat—were always obedient—would always show their asses.

The men seemed to believe that their women should always go-braless. Helen didn't see one woman in the whole place who seemed to have a bra on. Some of the men had tattoos—usually the Harley Davidson symbol.

Helen saw one small girl—one woman—with a red rose tattoo nearly the size of a lemon or tangerine in her cleavage. She wondered what kind of woman would agree to be tattooed where everyone could see it—always.

Helen and her girlfriend weren't approached directly, but the bartender gave them a cold shoulder and they were made to feel distinctly unwelcome. They were straight. City women, wearing designer jeans, in a biker bar, with Helen's barely two-year-old Jeep Grand Cherokee parked outside.

Helen didn't care. She nursed her beer and watched the men and the pool games and how the women acted and their obscene interplay between the bikers and their women. One of the men eventually came over to her. Helen sensed a pick-up. She was prepared to tell him to get lost, but she remembered that this was their place and she was the one who could be told to leave.

She looked at the biker as he walked up her. 30-ish, jeans, black t-shirt, denim vest with Frank across the left top, He looked like he lifted weights—what did they call them? Iron workers?—she didn't quite remember. He was all chest and biceps. Dark brown hair—she couldn't see easily in the glare of the bar lights, maybe black; it fell nearly to his shoulders. He looked cleaner than the others and carried himself with an air of—what? command? She didn't quite know. But she did notice he seemed slightly different than the rest. Cleaner, bigger, stronger with an air of command or authority—she couldn't tell. But he did appear to be different.

"Slummin', babe?" He leaned on the bar with his back, surveying the scene, looking sideways at her. She felt suddenly vulnerable and small.

She tried to ignore him, but his presence was too much. She had to say something.

"Just having a beer. That all right?"

"Sure babe—want to see how the other half lives? You and your girlfriend?"

Helen's friend had drifted away to make their conversation private.

"Maybe."

He took a swig of beer from a long-neck bottle.

"This is a long way from town—you picked a hell of a place to get a beer…"

She tried to silence him with a bitchy answer, but she couldn't think of any.

"You aren't from Oakland, are you babe?"

"No. San Francisco."

He appeared surprised.

"Jeez. Across the Bay. You come all this way for a beer?"

"Maybe."

"Had to get out of the city and away from all the fruits and nuts, huh? All the pretty boys," he asked sarcastically.

She tried to think of something to say—she didn't know how to talk to this man at all.

"You don't like San Francisco?"

"Hell no. Its' a gay town—not a man's town. Oakland is for men. 'Frisco—" he used the abbreviation which San Francisco residents didn't care for. "—is for all the gay boys." He put his beer on the bar, turned around, put his elbows on the bar and looked directly at her.

"You like the gay boys or real men?"

She enjoyed the challenge of this man—who seemed so obviously to know what he liked and what he didn't.

"I like men—not boys."

"I wonder," he said, and motioned the bartender for another beer. The bartender brought two and put one in front of Helen. She hadn't finished the one she was holding.

"Is this a pickup?"

"Do you want to be picked up?"

She looked carefully at the cold beer.

"No."

He shrugged. "Up to you."

She felt relieved, that this man wouldn't try to hustle her to bed. She felt relieved that she could talk to him without somehow worrying that he might try to rape her.

"All the others have nicknames—I've seen Magoo and Charger Charlie—and Muther—how come your vest only says Frank?"

He looked at her with renewed interest.

"Used to be Furious Frank, but Frank is good enough."

Helen tried to think of something else to say— something to ask that wouldn't mean she was terribly interested in all those guys—but she was, somehow.

"This seems to be a small club—only about a dozen of you in that club?"

"Los Gatos? No. Slow night. Most are home crashing—with their old ladies. They don't all show up unless we have a run." He turned around again so he could watch the whole bar.

"A run?"

"Ya, when we're on the road—then everyone's here. Together—ya know?"

Crissy appeared and nudged her and whispered. "I have to go home."

Helen turned to Frank.

"Got to go." He shrugged.

"Don't get raped by the pretty boys in 'Frisco—"
She climbed off the bar stool.

He turned to her again. "Come back sometime babe. You won't get raped unless you want it."

Helen left without a word. But she wondered about the bikers and their bikes and that nightclub and all the obscene t-shirts and all their nicknames and she wondered about their women and how the bikers treated their women and if they did rape straight women—and the next weekend she want back. Alone.

When she got back to the club, the next Saturday afternoon, she counted about the same number of men and about the same number of women. She sat at the bar. The bartender automatically brought her a cold bottle of beer. Since she had been talking to Frank the week before, apparently she was now OK. The bartender wasn't as frosty and stand-offish has he had been the first time. When she finished the beer, the bartender brought a second.

"Frank here?"

"Just left. He ought to be back."

Helen was disappointed. She wanted to talk with him and not be hassled by any of the others. Most of them were far dirtier—grungier—than Frank was—

she thought she could talk to him easier than she could to some of the rest. Some of the bikers—Magoo—The Animal—and some of the others looked like they were on the verge of—of what?—going stark-crazy at any minute. On the verge of being just stone crazy. Frank had appeared at least to be reasonable.

She waited and watched. She was again fascinated with the biker "colors,"—the vests they wore with the snarling panther on the back and their own names on the front and the t-shirts which were so obscene. They seemed to live amiably with the worst kind of obscenities and didn't mind at all. Some of them seemed grosser than others. Some of the guys, she suspected, lived for being gross and crude. Others just lived with it as a matter of lifestyle. It was such a new world for her, such a complete 180-degree turnabout from her straight world and the world of the gay men in San Francisco—she wanted to ask Frank about it all.

If he would tell her about it.

She nursed her beer slowly. She didn't want to get drunk here—alone. She didn't quite know what might happen to her. She wanted to stay sober. She might have had more to drink if she could trust Frank to behave. But she didn't want to drink too much alone—without him. If she could trust him.

He finally walked into the bar. She had heard

the roar of a cycle outside—or what they called a chopper. He was wearing much the same clothes. Levis, his vest, just like the week before. He saw her at the bar and walked over.

"Back again, babe?"

She nodded.

"Want another taste of real men? Not like all the boys in 'Frisco—?"

She didn't know what to say. He seemed always on the verge of teasing her because she lived in San Francisco, had a straight job and worked with some guys who were gay.

"Maybe."

"Maybe," he echoed and nodded for a beer.

"I heard a bike outside. Was that yours?"

He nodded again.

"Is it a Harley too?"

He seemed to smile, like she had made a private joke.

"I'd rather walk than ride a Jap bike. Sure it's a Harley. Ever ridden a good chopper?"

"No."

He finished his beer and tossed a couple dollars on the bar.

"Come on, I'll give you a ride. Put something hot and throbbing between your legs for a change."

She pondered. "Is it safe?"

He looked at her, smiling again. Cool. Mancho-man, she thought.

"If you want to be safe," he emphasized, "go home and play with your gay boys across the Bay—"

"OK," she said, "for a while."

They walked toward the door. One of the bikers playing pool shouted at Frank.

"New pussy tonight, Frank?"

Frank turned toward him—walked over, put his hand on the biker's shoulder and whispered something in his ear. Helen wondered what he said. The biker said nothing—shrugged and went back to his pool game.

"Who was that?"

"Gypsy Jerry," Frank said and offered nothing more about the biker.

Frank's motorcycle was nearby. Helen had never seen such a motorcycle—close up. It had wide handlebars, a massive chrome engine, and chrome gas tank with the Harley eagle on it and *Frank* in script across one side. All the engine parts seemed to Helen to be chrome. It has a two-step seat—the back seat raised and the front wheel was farther to the front than she expected it to be.

She as glad she worn her levis. It would have been impossible to straddle that motorcycle in any kind of skirt—long or short.

"Get on," Frank said casually. He flipped the kick-stand up and the engine rumbled to life and Frank gunned one of the handlebar grips causing the engine to roar. Helen had never heard such an enormous roar so close-up. She tentatively got on behind him and wondered how she could hold on.

Frank turned. "Hold my waist." He guided one hand around to his belt. She looked for some place to put her feet and found two small pegs. She pulled at his shoulder.

"That OK?" He nodded and before she could say anything else, he gunned the handlebars and the cycle jumped. They were out of the parking lot before Helen could think and were down the highway before she could take a deep breath.

"My God," she thought. The wind blew furiously through her hair, the cycle made an awful roar and she could barely see—the wind was making her eyes water. Her eyes closed against the wind. The cycle roared under her. It *did* throb.

She felt like she was riding an obscene beast. Something from hell. Rocketing down the highway. She held tight to Frank's waist. She was afraid to even lean when the bike went around curves. She hoped her weight wouldn't change how the cycle behaved.

She was fascinated and scared at the same time. She felt that she was somehow riding an iron beast with fire coming out of its behind; a modern dinosaur roaring down the road; some primeval monster roaring, snarling, barely under Frank's control (although she trusted his skill on the cycle.) The wind whipped her sleeves and blew her blonde hair. The roar of the engine was constant. Frank stopped at a stop sign once and let the engine idle. Even when it was idling it had an muffled roar; she felt the whole cycle throb under her and she felt the faint heat from the engine and the weight as it shifted under her.

"Doin' OK?" he asked her, over his shoulder.

She tied to nod—he couldn't see her.

"Yes. OK." He popped the handlebar and the front wheel jumped. She had to hold on even tighter—the chopper seemed to leap forward like a—well, like a snarling panther (and appropriate name for the club, she thought.) The cycle was a snarling panther.

Frank slowly drove through a suburban shopping center and Helen was surprised at how the people looked at them. She saw looks of fear and disgust and of fear and she saw people who clearly thought Frank—and her—for she was part of it to—were outlaws who ought to be locked up for disturbing the peace in front of their neighborhood Walmart.

Then they were out again and she was amazed how fast the cycle took the road. And how loud. She thought of an old country song she had heard years back, about speeding in a 1950s sedan: *the telephone poles looked like a picket fence*. Well, they did.

Frank was going so fast the telephone poles flashed by like a picket fence. Frank took the Expressway toward San Francisco and she was amazed how it felt—how fast and how free it was to be on his chopper.

Across the brides into San Francisco, Frank

idled the chopper through the Fisherman's Wharf area, then back across into Oakland—she had never seen the Bay so clearly—she had always been inside a car—protected by the windshield and all the steel and in where it was so quiet. Here she was exposed, the wind whipping constantly at her hair and clothes, the roar and throb of the engine under her was enormous and she saw the sights better than she had ever seen them before.

She was unhappy when they got back to the Roamin' Eye—she didn't want the ride to end. She was so fascinated with the chopper and how it behaved and what it felt like when she was holding Frank's belt and how the engine roared under her. It was a kind of freedom. To be on the road on a big Harley! She did like it Frank was a pro at it. She did like something hot and throbbing between her legs. And she did enjoy it! Every second of it.

She couldn't wait for the next week to end. Her job was so mundane—her colleagues so uninteresting. She longed to tell them what a fantastic ride she had, but she didn't. They wouldn't understand. They would think she was crazy to associate with *those bikers*.

Well, the hell with them! She knew when she had a good time. The ride was so thrilling—she couldn't wait to go back. She hoped Frank would give her another ride. She found him exciting—in a way none of the men she had ever met had excited her. He was so in command of the Harley and himself and the people around him. She was caught up in the biker mystique and she couldn't wait to get some more of it.

On the home from work one night, she stopped at a tourist shop, a quick-print on Fisherman's Wharf and looked around. She thought she might have a t-shirt custom made for herself. She found a scoop-neck blue t-shirt and she had the shop hot-press a biker on it, with the phrase *Harleys Forever* in script across the bottom. She bought a matching headscarf. She wanted a black motorcycle jacket, but she didn't know where to shop for one. Maybe Frank could help her get one.

She got to the Roamin'Eye early Friday night. There were a few bikers around. By this time, the bartender knew her well enough put a cold bottle of beer in front of her when she sat down at the bar, without making it seem like she was in the wrong bar, alone. She asked him where Frank was—he told her that he expected Frank in later. So she sat at the bar and waited and nursed her beer and played pinball. She declined an invitation from a biker to play pool. "I'm waiting for someone," she said.

Frank finally arrived. She wondered if she could recognize the sound of his cycle. She heard several roar into the parking lot. They all sounded the same. When Frank walked in, she was surprised. And relieved. He didn't seem surprised to see her. She was wearing the t-shirt and the scarf, designer jeans and boots.

"Can't stay away, babe?" he sat down beside her. He bartender brought him a beer.

"I thought—= I thought—maybe you could take me for another another ride—

He looked at her carefully. "Maybe, babe—"

"I loved it so—and I want to get a jacket. A cycle jacket—but I don't know where or what kind—can you help me?"

It sounded to her almost like she was making a play for him—and maybe she was—but it was sincere—she did want a biker's jacket. In black leather, in her own size and she did want his help in telling her where to get one.

"Sure babe—that's easy. I own a bike shop. We've got 'em in stock your size."

She was thrilled. "Well, can I get one? When? Will you take a check? If you have them, I'd like another couple of t-shirts. This one—" she gestured aimlessly at her chest, "isn't terrific. I'd like a really nice one. Or two."

"Sure. I'll take you over. Finish your beer."

She drank the rest of her beer and put a couple of bills on the bar. Frank finished his, dropped a bill onto the bar and they walked outside. Frank got on his cycle, kicked the kickstand and turned on the engine. She was always thrilled when the engine roared to life. She got on the backseat and held his waist.

He gunned the handlebars so the bike's front wheel jumped off the ground, eased onto the highway and drove away from Oakland. Helen was thrilled again when the wind caught her clothes, when she heard the muffled roar—the distinct sound of a Harley exhaust, and felt the deep throb of the cycle between her legs.

She turned her head to the side, pressed her chest against the heavy back of Frank's motorcycle jacket and watched the fences and the roadway blur by. It was so fast! So thrilling! And she did have something hot and throbbing between her legs. And a real man in front of her!

Frank drove out farther into the country, out of Oakland, away from the Bay area. He began slowing, as the bike began a long curve. Then he pulled off the road into a parking lot. She saw a two-story concrete block building, neat and trim. *The Chopper Shop* above the door.

She saw Harley Davidson posters inside, and some bikes inside the dark and closed shop. Frank parked the bike and went to a side door. He took a ring of keys, opened the door and turned on the lights. She walked through a repair area, with grease and oil on the floor, past shelves of parts, toward the front of the shop, which had about eight used choppers for sale, racks of t-shirts and black leather jackets. Frank turned on the lights in front of the building, walked to a rack and pulled a jacket from a hangar. "Try it."

Helen tried it on. Too big.

She tried on another. It fit better. A third fit perfectly. She didn't care what the price was—she wanted this jacket. Black and shiny—the leather smelled good and creaked slightly. She loved the feel of the leather. It had zippers up the sleeves nearly to the elbows, and down the front. She felt like a biker in it. She wrote Frank a check and left the amount and the Pay To: part blank. She gave him the check. "You fill it out to The Chopper Shop," he said, so she did and gave him the check back. "Want to see my ID? My driver's license?"

"Nope," he said, "if the check's no good, I'll rape you instead." Helen didn't know quite if he was joking or not.

He walked to a hangar full of t-shirts. "Pick one out."

She found her size and took a black women's t with a beautiful flying eagle on it in gold. Across the top it said *Harley Davidson*. Across the bottom, *Made in America*. She couldn't wait to try it on.

"Want to see the rest of the place?"

"Sure."

She followed him through the back of the shop, to wooden staircase. He flipped a light switch then walked up the stairs and opened a door. She followed.

The second floor was a loft apartment with a beamed ceiling. On the left was a alley kitchen, then a double bed against the wall. A sofa nearby and a small TV on a table. A door led to a bathroom, she imagined,

On the right side of the loft was an empty space—fully half the loft was empty.

On that side, three pulleys were hung from a beam in the ceiling. On the floor an assortment of ropes and chains lay in a pile. She wondered about that. But she thought that Frank and his friends carried cycles up here, or part of them and hung them so they could be worked on. Odd, she thought, but maybe he liked to work here instead of downstairs. There were no windows—the entire loft was lit by lights in the ceiling. It wasn't much, but a nice apartment above the cycle shop. And it was quiet. None of the highway noises could be heard up here. A nice place to live if you owned the shop, she thought, then told Frank so.

He lit a cigarette, then sat on the sofa, near the bed. A few bikers magazines were on the floor. A man's place, she thought. Could use some cleaning.

She didn't know quiet what to say. She sat demurely on the sofas and lit a cigarette of her own. He reached to the floor, picked up an ashtray and put it on the sofa between them.

"Your club—The Los Gatos—can anyone join?"

He looked at her.

"Anyone who has a chopper and wants to, can join."

"How about women?"

He paused.

"You don't know much about bikers. *Men* (he emphasized it) join. If they have an old lady—they come along. Women don't' have their own bikes. If a member has an old lady, fine if not—" He paused.

"So women bikers can't join by themselves?"

"The only women bikers I have seen are the college kids who have Jap bikes—Hondas and Yamahas and whatnot. No real chopper rider is—" He corrected himself. "Women don't ride choppers, except in back. Bikers who ride have their mommas. Their old ladies—"

She wondered if she was going too far with this man. She looked at the zipper on the left sleeve of her leather jacket.

"Do you have an old lady?

"Used to—she split. Went home to her momma probably." He said it casually, as though the story wasn't worth telling.

She wanted to go on, but didn't quite know how.

"Do you have any beer?"

"Sure." He said and got two cans from the refrigerator in the kitchen area. He came back and handed her one can, kept the other.

"I—" she said, "I'd like to join your club. If I can—somehow—you said—"

He turned to her.

"You can join if you have an old man who's

a biker. You don't know about bikers. You'll have to burn your bridges behind you. Biker women do exactly what they are told to do. What their old man wants. When he wants it. There's no Women's Lib, no outside jobs, no 'honey I to want do—' and no (he emphasized) *'I don't want to do this'* or *'I won't do this—'*" The biker lays down the law. It takes a special woman to be a biker babe. A lot of women think they'll live with a biker—then discover they can't They are either with their man or they split. It's a heavy commitment. Think it over."

And he added an afterthought. "And no kids dragging along with their momma."

"Is that why—did your (she tried to use his phrase) old lady split—because she couldn't handle it?'

"Something like that."

She drank her beer, thinking.

"Try your t-shirt on," he said suddenly.

"Okay, where's your bathroom?" He pointed to the door she had thought led to a bathroom. She walked into the bathroom, took off her new jacket, and t-shirt she had bought, and put on her new one. Her new one was much nicer than the one she had bought for herself. She tucked the t into her jeans and walked out, carrying her jacket by the collar in one hand. She stood in front of him.

"Like it?"

She thought it was terrific. It was just tight

enough to show off her breasts.

"Fine, sure," he said without much enthusiasm.

"Most biker women don't wear bras. 'fact is, none of them wear bras. Try it without your bra."

She wanted to hesitate, but then said nothing and walked back to the bathroom. She pulled off the t-shirt, took off her bra, pulled the t-shirt back on and tucked it into her jeans and stuffed the bra into a ball. She'd put it in her jacket pocket in a minute.

"Like it better?"

He looked at her. She felt different without her bra in front of this man.

"Sure," he said, getting up. "That's better."

He began walking to the stairs leading down to the shop. She tagged along behind him.

"You miss having an old lady?" she asked, wondering if she wasn't treading on thin ice.

"Sometimes," he said, without turning back toward her. "Sure."

She was again thrilled on the drive back to the bar, as the cycle roared through the night, an iron monster with fire spitting out behind. She held onto Frank hard, and buried her face in the back of his jacket, the wind grabbing at her. She felt different without a bra, more vulnerable somehow. She wondered if any of the other bikers in the bar would notice she wasn't wearing a bra. She though they'd probably notice—if anything—her new biker jacket. She wondered what Frank's previous woman was like.

She hated to leave when the bar closed. Frank had made no move to seduce her—she wondered about that. She wanted to wear her leather jacket to work, but knew everyone would wonder about it. She could carry fashion only so far at work—she was expected to wear women's business suits. Slacks or pant suits were not allowed. There was no official policy, but no one ever wore pants suits. Helen wanted to wear her designer jeans and the t-shirt Frank had given her and her new black jacket, just to show everyone up, but she knew she shouldn't. So she called in sick one morning during the week and drove out to Frank's cycle shop.

He was busy inside repairing an old chopper. He might have been surprised to see her, but if he was, he didn't show it. His hands were dirty and he worn an old torn t-shirt and greasy jeans. Bikers came and went. Helen had brought a thermos of coffee with her. There was another biker working at the shop and while Frank was busy, she bought another t-shirt from him. A gold t with the phrase *Born for Fun, Loyal to None* below a biker on a roaring cycle.

She was disappointed that he didn't interrupt his work to talk to her. She browsed around and finally got mad at him for ignoring her.

She walked over to where he was down on one knee, repairing the old cycle.

"Don't you say anything to a customer?"

He looked up.

"Busy. This one needs a valve job."

"Too busy to say hello?" she stood over him, with her legs apart, challenging him. She had her new jacket on and he had ignored her.

"Too busy right now."

She watched him as a wrench he held slipped and gashed his knuckles.

"Serves you right," she said. She felt like she used to, when she was so bitchy to her mama and to her younger sister and to the college boys who wanted to get into her panties.

"Up yours, bitch," he said, without looking at her.

She left, without speaking and was so mad on the drive back to San Francisco she thought she would weep. She was terrible at work the rest of the week. Most of the boys she worked with—the gay ones—thought she was bitchy because she was having her period. "You poor dear," one sympathized to her. But somehow she couldn't wait to get back to the Roamin' Eye the next weekend, to see if Frank was there, to see if he would apologize to her, or if he would take her for another ride on his chopper.

She couldn't wait to see Frank the next weekend: she wanted to see him and ride—it was so exciting to have that great roaring machine under her and feel the wind in her hair and watch the road go flashing past—she loved all of it. But she also wanted to give him a good piece of her mind—she had taken a whole day off work and drove all the way out to see him and he couldn't be bothered because he was fixing some old chopper. Who did he think he was talking to? She was irritated at the mere thought of how he had treated her.

She left her apartment early Friday afternoon. She wore a sweater, her designer jeans which hugged her behind so tightly and a pair of tan boots. She knew she was attractive; 25 years old. 35 B or C cup (she was between a 34 and a 36 and between a B and a C) 35 or so–24–36-and-one-half. Her designer jeans showed off her behind. She knew it. She had seen men watch her. Her behind and her legs were her best features.

She wore her hair in a fashionable shag cut—it was ash blonde—almost a dirty blonde, She loved her biker jacket. The leather jacket she had bought from Frank. The leather smelled so wonderful and it creaked when she moved, it was so new. It made her feel good.

Powerful, exciting. And it always reminded her of riding behind Frank, on his chopper and how good that made her feel. She looked forward to riding on the back of his bike, her hair in the wind, her arms around his waist. She had felt the bulge in his levis—he was all man—she knew it. It was only a matter of time until he was in love with her.

Until he wanted her to be his biker girl.

His "old lady," although she was hardly old.

She drove to the Roamin' Eye—and hoped he would be there. She expected him to apologize for mistreating her—when she had taken the day off earlier and driven all that way to see him. All he had done was work on that old chopper and gash his knuckles doing it. He would apologize—she knew it.

She got to the Roamin' Eye early. There were only a few choppers parked outside. She felt like she belonged there—with her biker jacket on. She walked in and the bartender put a cold bottle of beer in front of her. She looked around.

A few members of the club were playing pool, or pinball or talking with their biker girls. The women were dressed like the men—they all wore levis and boots and either t-shirts (usually with the Harley Davidson eagle on them) or denim vests. The women largely ignored her. That was alright.

None of them were as attractive as she was. The men seemed to knows he was Frank's girl, so they ignored her too. Later, she knew, they would warm up to her. Occasionally a few more bikers roared into the parking lot.

Each time she expected to see Frank—she was unhappy she couldn't tell the sound of his motorcycle from all the others—they all sounded alike.

Finally, he got there. Helen was idly talking to

the bartender. She didn't realize he was there. He just came in and sat down beside her.

"Frank!"

"How you doin'?"

"I—OK—" She didn't know quite what to say. She wanted to make him feel badly for not paying attention to her a few days earlier, but she was surprised that he didn't just say anything more. That he didn't immediately apologize to her.

"I drove over the other day and you just ignored me. I spent the whole day and you just worked on that old motorcycle."

He shrugged. "Should have called first." He took a long drink of his beer.

"Well," she said, haughtily, "I think you ought to apologize for ignoring me—"

He spun around on his barstool, and surveyed the crowd. His beer held in his lap. Then he suddenly turned to her and held her by the nape of her neck.

"That's not the way it works, bitch. Not now. Not ever. I don't apologize to any bitch for anything."

She was incensed.

"But I—"

"But what, babe?" He still held her by the nape of her neck.

"But what?" repeated. His hands hurt her.

"Stop Frank, you're hurting me."

He let go of her neck and grabbed her by her hair, and shook her head back and forth. She yipped with the pain.

"Frank!"

She hoped the bartender would make him stop. She thought that everyone would be watching them. Then she thought that everyone would be horrified how he was treating her. Her head still hurt. But no one was paying any attention. At all. The bikers were playing pool or pinball or talking with their women. The bartender was at the other end of the bar, talking with another biker. No ones thought anything at all out of the ordinary when he pulled her hair so. He finally let go of her hair.

They sat in silence for a moment.

"That's the way it is, babe," he said, casually.

She sat, hurt and felt mistreated. The rest of the evening Frank talked to her, or talked to his friends, or drank beer and shot pool with his buddies. She sat at the bar or watched him play pool. She still expected him to apologize for the few days before, when he had ignored her or *at least* apologize for grabbing her by her hair, but he didn't do either.

As far as he was concerned, she thought, those incidents never existed. He showed no sign he'd apologize for either incident.

About one a.m., he turned to her. They were both sitting at the bar. She had had about four beers, he more than six.

"Let's go."

"Where?"

"To my place."

"I've got my car outside."

"Leave it here or drive it down. It'll be OK here, or you can park it behind my shop."

She wanted so much to ride behind him in on his chopper, but she didn't want to leave her car behind. No telling what might happen to it and she'd have all the hassle of an insurance claim.

"I'll drive behind you."

He shrugged. "OK, babe, let's go."

She followed him to his place. He drove faster than she could drive her car in the dark. He weaved in and out of traffic—when she had to stay in one lane. It was lucky she had been to his place before, or she would have lost him in traffic and never found her way to his cycle shop and his loft above it.

When she got to his shop, the parking lot was deserted. There was only one light on a highway pole, many yards away. Only occasionally did a lone car drive past. She parked as far as she could, off the road toward the edge of his shop.

She saw him waiting at the backdoor. He had apparently pulled his chopper into the work area. The light was already on inside. Well, his chopper was so expensive, she would have parked it inside if it had been hers. But it was too big for her to ride—she's need a small size Harley.

"Let's go, babe." He said and suddenly picked her up, swung her over his shoulders and carried her up the stairs like a side of beef. She hung upside down, her head hanging down his back.

"Frank. Frank. Let me down."

He held her by the backs of her knees. She tried to kick and struggle, but her only smacked her hard on her behind.

Upstairs, in the loft, he put her down. She was flushed from being carried upside down.

He just grinned at her. She had expected him to apologize for carrying her so rudely, but he said nothing. She began to realize he wouldn't apologize to her for *anything*.

So she smoothed down her sweater and pulled her jacket straight. He shrugged off his biker jacket and tossed it on the floor, missing a chair. He came over to her and slid his hands under the sides of her sweater.

"Want to be my biker bitch?"

She was surprised. That was more like it. He would have to ask her and ask her—she would say *yes*, eventually—but he's have to know she was in charge.

"Maybe," she sniffed.

He slid his hands farther, up under her sweater, then suddenly picked her up and walked to the bed. He dropped her on the bed, pulled her legs up and pulled her boots off. He reached for her waist, unbuckled her belt and unzipped her jeans. He pulled them off.

"Frank!"

He looked at her, then walked across the room to turn off the stairway light. Then he recrossed the room and turned on the light in the bathroom, leaving a crack of light across the floor.

"Get undressed babe. Now."

She watched him start to pull his boots off. Well, she would get undressed, but she'd make sure later he wouldn't treat her like this again. She sat up, pulled off her leather jacket and dropped it on the floor. She pulled her sweater off and dropped it on her jacket.

She bent both arms behind her and unhooked her bra and let it fall on the pile of her sweater and jacket. He had been watching her.

He had everything off except his levis, standing about four feet in front of her. She was down to her panties. She lifted her behind off the bed and pulled the covers down. The bed looked like it hadn't been made in days. She pulled the covers up, slid her panties off, tried to discreetly drop them on the pile of clothes and laid back with the covers almost up to her neck

He was undressed. She could see in the half light that he was fully erect. Or nearly so. He got in bed beside her. His fingers found her slit. Then inside her. Immediately. She didn't know if she would be wet or what. She felt his fingers exploring inside her. She wanted him to be slow. She wanted him to ask for it. She expected him to ask her to make love. But he said nothing. He lifted her butt off the bed by the fingers in her slit. Then again. And again. She felt him roll on top of her.

AAAAAHHH! He slid fully inside her. She was wet enough, but he was too fast. He pulled her knees up, almost to her breasts, then held them there by wrapping his arms around her legs, behind her knees. She felt her butt tip toward him. She wrapped her arms around his back. So strong. She felt the muscles in his back. He wasn't making love to her—he wasn't raping her. Just something in between. He was simply, steadily, screwing her. Thrusting and thrusting, holding her down on the bed. He lifted himself up off her and held the soles of her feet. She couldn't see his face in the dark. She reached for him, but couldn't touch him.

"Frank—" He said nothing. The only contact she had with him was his thing, his big thing inside her, his hands holding the soles of feet, her legs up.

"Frank—You're not making love—too fast—I—"

He let go of her, turned her over and made her get onto her hands and knees. He slid into her again from behind, and held her by both hips. She felt him thrusting and thrusting inside her.

"Frank," she said, more insistently, "you're just screwing me."

"That's right babe," he said, then grabbed her hair and pulled her head back.

"That's right babe."

Her head hurt. She thought he might he might

pull her hair out by the roots.

"That's right babe. Just an old-fashioned screwing. I think you need more of it."

He held her even tighter by the hair; She aw white sparks behind her eyes.

"Oouuuwww. Frank. Ooooww. Alright. Just screw me."

"Say please."

The pain was too great.

"Alright Frank. Screw me."

"Again."

"Screw me Frank. Do it harder. Do it any way you want. Just fuck me."

She felt indignant saying what he wanted her to say.

She felt humiliated.

And wet.

Wetter than she ever had been before.

Humiliated, submissive and wet. All at once.

"That's better. Now don't you feel better?"

"No, Frank—I—"

He yanked again.

"Don't Frank, you're raping me"

"Don't you like it this way?"

He eased the tension on her hair and head ever so slightly.

"No—YES—Frank—" She knew he wouldn't stop until she said what he wanted to hear.

"Yes. Frank, fuck me. Just fuck me hard."

"One more time. Get it right."

"Fuck me, Frank. Just fuck me hard."

He let go of her hair, then turned her onto her back again and continued to steadily screw her. Suddenly he rolled off her. "Down." He pushed her head down.

"Frank—I—"

He was more insistent. "Down."

She slid down and took his cock in her hand.

"Suck it, pussy."

She never liked this. She almost never did that for any of he college boys she had dated.

"NOW."

She didn't want him to pull her hair. She put his wet thing in her mouth.

"Suck it." She began to bob her head up and down, sliding his thing in and nearly out of her mouth. He lightly held the back of her head.

"Faster." She bobbed her head up and down, obediently faster.

He pushed her head down until his cock was completely in her mouth and held her head down.

His erect thing was completely in her mouth. As nearly completely as she could manage.

"Now bitch." She had to breathe through her nose carefully.

His cum splashed into her mouth, again and again, his hot bitter come. It had been years, since a man had done this to her. Now this man would probably do it as if he had every right. She gagged once. And gagged again. She wanted to spit out his cum. But he held her head down. He had shot five spurts of his cum into her mouth—and he had no intention of letting her up yet.

"Swallow, bitch."

She tried to struggle. *Mmmmmmm MMMMMMMM.*

He jammed her head down. Her nose was buried in his public hair. but she finally swallowed him, as much as she could. He must have felt her swallowing. He finally let her up.

She sat up and wiped her mouth. She began to get up.

"Where you going?"

"To the bathroom. I want to wash my mouth—"

He grabbed her, swung her around and smacked her butt. Hard.

"Lie down. You're alright." He pulled her back onto the bed and swung one leg over her.

"You're not going to be poisoned. Don't you dare get up. You can spend the night without washing your mouth. You ought to be pleased to have my come in your mouth. Can't you say 'thank you?'"

She didn't want him to do anything more to her.

"Ok, thank you Frank," she said flatly.

"For what? Say it."

"Thank you for coming in my mouth. I enjoyed it."

But she hadn't enjoyed it much. He had almost raped her. She hadn't been anywhere near her own climax. He had simply taken her and nearly raped her and then held her head down and spurted his stuff into her mouth.

"Say it like you mean it."

"Thank you Frank—" She knew now to say more than she wanted to. Much more.

"Thank you Frank. I hope you liked fucking me. You're so strong. You just fucked and fucked me. And I hope you liked cuming in my mouth."

"That's better. No don't you dare get up—" She tried to settle back on the bed.

He suddenly spread his legs wide, almost throwing her hips off the bed.

"Get down. I want you to sleep between my legs. Curl up."

"Frank—I can't—I—"

He got up on one elbow then leaned over her.

"You don't say no to me. Not now. Not ever."

He grabbed her hair again and twisted it in his fist.

"Understand?'

She tried to look into his eyes.

"Alright," she said, quietly. Then she crawled down and curled up between his legs.

"Alright, Frank."

He pulled the covers up over her. She smelled his masculine muskiness and semen in his groin. He said something she couldn't understand clearly under the covers. She relaxed and fell asleep.

Helen awoke. She didn't know where she was. Under covers. In a bed. She remembered. How Frank and nearly raped her. How he made her take his thing in her mouth. Then how he came in her mouth. And not let her wash her mouth after. And made her sleep between his legs. She still had his taste in her mouth. She slowly pulled herself up. He was still asleep. She didn't know what time it was—there were no windows in the loft. She didn't try to get up—she didn't know what he would do if he got up and she was already up. She tried as carefully as she could, to stretch, to get the cramps out of her legs, from being doubled up for—for how long? She knew he would want to find her curled up as he told her. So she slid back down into the bed again and dozed off again. She finally felt him move. Then he moved again and she was sure he must be was awake. She crawled up again. He was awake.

"You almost raped me last night."

"Almost babe."

"You hurt me."

"Where babe? You cut? Bruised? Beaten? Where? Show me."

Well, it wasn't visible, he hadn't beaten her up.

"You hurt me, Frank. You pulled my hair."

"You look alright now."

"Well, you hurt me."

She sensed he was getting angry at her.

"Lighten up babe."

"Well you *did* hurt me."

"Let it go now. NOW." He got up and pulled on a pair of levis. She didn't know men just wore levis without anything on under them.

She got up and reached for her panties.

"You look alright to me." He walked over and smacked her butt. "It was just what you needed, wasn't it?"

She looked at him.

"No."

He smacked her butt harder. Her behind burned. She thought it might be burning red just from the two smacks.

"Yes, alright Frank. It was just fine. Thank you. I hope you loved it."

She knew she had to be even more explicit.

"Hope you liked using my pussy and mouth."

"That's better."

He watched her put on her panties and her jeans.

"That's enough. Let me see you. Make some coffee."

"Frank—I—" He smacked her again. Hard. It hurt even though her jeans. So she made coffee for the two of them, wearing nothing but her jeans. She sat barefooted and topless sipping her hot coffee while he watched her.

"You're just fine babe. What are your measurements? You may have told me."

He reached over the kitchen table and played with her left nipple, nudging it with his thumb and forefinger, then cupped her left breast with his hand and lightly shook it.

"I don't remember if I did. I'm hard to fit. It's hard to find a perfect bra. I'm between bra sizes, bigger than a 34, not quite a 36. And between a B cup and a C cup. If I find a bra that fits I usually don't like the design. And underwire bras are painful to wear. Did you know that?" She suspected he didn't have a clue about underwire bras.

They finished the coffee and he got dressed the rest of the way. He let her shower quickly and brush her teeth and get dressed. They took a long, long ride on his chopper all day and she loved every minute of it.

They ate at a roadside steak-and-beer restaurant and finally got back to his place at dark. They had a couple of beers apiece, then he picked her up and carried her to the bed. This time he had her take off her clothes in front of him in the light. Then he screwed her again.

He didn't make her ask for it—but she told him "Just fuck me." Because she knew he wanted her to say it. She was more obedient and he didn't rape her quite as hard as the night before. But he held her head down again until she swallowed his climax and again he made her sleep cured up naked between his legs.

Helen took some clothes with her the next weekend. She stayed with Frank during the weekends and went back to work early Monday mornings. She missed him in her apartment during the week. But she spent every weekend with him in his loft. She never asked what the pulleys on the ceiling were for—and the ropes that hung from them. She never saw them used for anything.

He was always the same. He didn't make love to her—he didn't seem to care about her own pleasure, her own climax. She hadn't had one climax of her own with him. He didn't rape her exactly, but he screwed her, he fucked and fucked her every night they were together. She didn't know a man could have so much stamina.

On top of her and doggie style—he put her on her hands and knees with her knees spread, and them told her to put her head down, arch her back and offer her pussy to him. Or on her knees and elbows, with her butt arched up and toward him and her head down.

Or completely face down, her breasts pressed flat, with a pillow under her hips, again to thrust her butt up toward him—to offer him her pussy and her legs spread. (He told her she was a very inviting piece of ass.)

And with her bent over a chair.

Then under him again. She was never on top.

She learned that she had to ask him to fuck her, to tell him how much she wanted it. Her pussy got sore, but she didn't tell him. Then her mouth got sore too and she didn't tell him that either.

She avoided getting her hair pulled or getting her butt smacked by always asking Frank to fuck her. During the weekends he closed his shop and they rode on his chopper exploring the country. She loved the long rides, with her biker jacket on, holding Frank's waist. They ate at small diners and cafes and she didn't mind at all.

During some early evenings, they spent hours at the Roamin' Eye and eventually she got to meet his friends. The bikers with the crazy names. Magoo, Mutha, The Animal. Some were bigger than Frank and many dirtier. All wore the same boots and levis and the vests with the Los Gatos name on the back. Helen didn't meet many of the bikers women. Frank explained that they didn't trust her yet. Helen didn't mind that—she was a man's woman, not a woman who had a lot of girl friends.

She woke one morning, warm and curled up between Frank's legs. She sneaked up out of the covers. There was something wrong. Something she knew was wrong. But what? They had done their usual screwing the night before and she knew that—what?—what day was it? Yesterday was Saturday. No—yesterday was Sunday. Sunday! This was Monday morning. She was late—she would be 'way late when she go to her office. She threw the covers off ands frantically began dressing. And all that drive into San Francisco—she'd be lucky if she got there by eleven or twelve. She—

Frank awoke.

"I'm late Frank. I have to be going. I have to be at work. I—"

He grabbed her by one elbow.

"No Frank, let me go. I have to go to work—"

"Don't bother. I called your office. Your business card was in your purse. I called them earlier. Told 'em you quit. You're going to live here now"

"You WHAT Frank?" She was astonished.

"You're going to live here now babe. You're going to be my biker chick. No going off to 'Frisco every Sunday night and comin' back on Fridays—"

"You bastard." Naked, Helen swung at him, aiming her fingernails at his face. Frank caught her arm, and twisted it behind her back. Even when he was naked and just waking up, she was no match for him. They struggled. He pinned her left arm up, up, behind her back so she had to stand on her tip-toes to avoid a terrible pain in her shoulders.

"Frank—you—I'll—" He pulled her over to the

side of the loft when the pulleys and ropes hung from the ceiling.

"You don't do anything, bitch. You're going to learn your manners starting now. Today. You'll sleep with me and work if I want you to work and when and where I want, and you'll stay here when I want and fuck and suck when I want it—"

Helen continued to struggle with him, but he held her firmly. Tightly, so she couldn't move. And then he tied her tightly, her arms behind her, then made her kneel and he tied her legs and ankles. Yards and Yards of rope. That was the day she spent so long with the ropes crisscrossed over and under her breasts, her arms bound from her wrists to her elbows.

She was naked on the floor, until he decided to let her stand. He pulled her panties down and off her legs. then he put a belt around her waist, and slid a rope from the pulleys between her legs and tied it to the belt at the center of her waist.

He pulled all the slack out of the rope—it tightened between her legs—it cut into her pussy so—deep into her slit and up between her butt cheeks. She spent hours and hours in pain, aching, constant pain, in her arms and legs and pussy and butt, but her pussy most of all. Frank finally let her down and she collapsed on the bed exhausted. She slept the rest of the day.

The next morning Frank let her get up without

tying her arms or legs. During the time she was asleep, he had brought an old steamer trunk into the loft and set it near the stairway door. There was a big padlock on it.

She discovered that he had locked all clothes in it. She spent the day wearing pair of panties and nothing else. He spent the day working in his shop, downstairs, locking the door to the loft when he left. Locking her in. He finally came up found her sitting cross-legged on the floor, reading an old biker magazine.

"What's your bra size? I'll bring you something tonight."

She was sure she had told him, but men forget some things like that. Women's sizes and such.

"Between a 34 and a 36. I'm a bit too big for a 34 and sometimes too small for a 36. And between a B and a C cup. Bras to fit me are hard to find. A 35 B cup if you can find any. They are usually 34 to 36—no 35s."

He nodded and left and when he left he locked the door again. Locking her in the loft.

Finally she heard his key in the loft door.

She had been dozing in bed, with the covers up around her shoulders. No TV in the loft and only a few bikers magazines. She had read through them all and then read them all again.

He nudged her shoulder.

"Got something for you, babe."

He seemed to have a department store bag.

"Try it on."

He held out the bag. She opened it—a black bra. A underwire push-up bra. 34 B. Underwires so her breasts would be pushed up and out and her cleavage pronounced. But she knew she had told him that underwire bras hurt. Then she thought—he bought that on purpose so when she was wearing it—the underwires would hurt. And a half size too small so her breasts would be even more on display. She felt entirely different when she put it on, with the top half of her breasts pushed up and exposed. The underwires began to cut into her and hurt almost immediately. She didn't tell him.

And then once she had to tell him something else.

She was in the loft, alone. Locked in. She wore a pair of white, low-cut panties, with a slight V in the front and back. Otherwise she was naked. She was terribly bored. No TV, no books, no radio, no windows—she had read the old bikers' magazines again and again and had them almost memorized. She had no clue what time it was or when Frank would be back.

She heard the key in the door lock.

"Frank? What time is it?"

"2:30. Afternoon. My mechanic can handle the

shop for a while. I thought I'd take a break."

He walked over to her and swirled a finger around her left nipple. Then he cupped her breast in his hand and shook it slightly.

"An afternoon break."

"Frank," she paused, "I never say no to you, but this isn't the time—"

"Got your period?

"No, it isn't that, but I'm dry. It wouldn't work now. "You couldn't get in me easy and it would hurt me."

"*Now*, pussy."

"Frank—I'd need some lubrication, oils, anything."

"I'll look around."

He left and locked the door.

He returned faster that she expected—he might have gone to the nearest convenience store for—something—even though men don't know much about how a woman stays lubricated.

"We have a shower and storage room behind the parts area. I found this."

A plastic tub of vasoline. A large tub, apparently never used.

I don't think this stuff ever gets too old, she thought to herself.

She got up from sitting on the bed, took the jar and began to walk away.

"Where you goin'?"

"To the bathroom."

He held her forearm.

"Do it here—you don't need to hide."

She went back to the bed, pulled down her panties, and opened the jar. It still seemed to be fresh.

She swirled some on a finger and wiped her pussy slowly.

"You need more than that. Fill your pussy. You got enough in that jar."

She then swabbed two fingers with vasoline and slowly inserted them into herself and swirled her fingers around. And again. And again. After the fourth time—with Frank watching—she said, "You too."

He stood next to the bed. She covered three fingers with vasoline and got down on her knees. He stepped in front of her. She slowly applied the vasoline to his cock, stroking it and making sure all it was covered.

"You wonder what it tastes like?" he asked her. "Try it."

It can't be all that bad, she thought to herself.

She ran her tongue back and forth across his cock—then swirled her tongue around his cockhead, ran her tongue up and down the underside of his cock. Then took it in her mouth. Slowly sucking him, back and forth, again and again.

"So? How is it?"

She held it in one hand.

"Just a slight waxy taste. Mostly just slick."

"Maybe we could get it in flavors. What flavor would you like?"

She hesitated for a split second.

"Dark chocolate. I like the taste of dark chocolate in my mouth."

She felt a flush of humiliation.

He couldn't miss the implication.

It was a taunt. Both of them knew it.

"How about some dark chocolate pussy?"

"Maybe sometime. You got any dark chocolate pussy nearby?"

"I could get some."

"Fresh young dark pussy. You'd like to watch, wouldn't you?"

He pulled her up. She then laid on her back in the bed, her legs spread, her knees slightly up.

"Here's your afternoon delight," she said.

He got between her spread legs and slowly entered her. But just half-way—

"That's the pussy you want. Go ahead."

He didn't lie on her. He held himself up by his arms.

"Pull your knees—up to your tits."

She was surprised—what position did he want?

"She lifted one leg as high as she could go, toward her right breast. Then the other leg.

"Point you feet at the ceiling."

She raised both feet. That was easier.

"Now put you ankles on my shoulders."

At the same time she did, he lowered himself onto her. And thrust completely into her.

Her ankles on his shoulders and his full weight on her, shifted her—her butt tipped up toward him. It seemed that her pussy was now *inviting* him to fuck her. He couldn't move under him—she was completely wrapped up in a ball and her butt continued to stay tipped up.

He entered her more deeply then—deeper than she had ever felt. That was a position for deep, deep penetration.

"You're totally in me—you can't get in me any deeper."

His thrusts were slow and continued as deep as possible. She couldn't struggle at all—she knew he was trying to make each thrust completely fill her. He crossed her arms over her head and held her wrists with hand. She couldn't get her ankles off his shoulders.

She then had a *very* bizarre idea that she could actually visualize—a physically impossible, but totally erotic thought—*if his stiff cock was much, much longer, it would go completely through me and out my open mouth.*

She didn't know how old the tub of vasoline was—but it worked—she was completely moist.

He was completely in her as deep as he could get—and he wanted to thrust even deeper.

She felt a strong surge of humiliation, but she told him what she had visualized.

"If your cock was much, much longer it could go completely through me—all the way up my belly and come out my open mouth."

He finally pulled away from her, her ankles slipped from his shoulders and her legs dropped down.

She crawled down and began to suck him. She wanted to suck him—take his cock as deep in her mouth—as deeply he had been fucking her.

His cum splashed into her mouth, spurting again and again—and when he came, and it went down her throat, she quivered with the first climax she had with him—and the most intense and longest climax she had ever had. In her life.

After that first time, he always took her in that position—with her legs up, her ankles on his shoulders, and her butt tipped toward him—offering her pussy to his cock. She often asked for it—she didn't want any other position. She always came then, total shuddering waves of intensity—from the deep, deep fucking he gave her.

"I always taste your cum in my mouth, for days and days—" she told him, "and I always smell semen on me. The taste and smell never go away. Before they fade away, you take me again."

Soon after that session, he told her, "you're just a total whore."

"I'm not," she said, "whores get paid."

"Some whores give it away—especially to men who think they should get some pussy any time they want.

"Don't you think you should be a total whore?"

She felt a warm wave of humiliation sweep through her.

"Just sometimes."

"You could be trained to become a complete whore."

"Are you going to try to train me?"

He did not answer.

She wondered what his answer might have been. She could not guess about him—or about that idea for her.

And the second she turned away, thinking the conversation was over, she got a hard smack on her butt.

"Think about it—a total whore 24-7 who gives it away to the man who expects to get pussy anytime he wants.

"A total whore."

"Maybe just sometimes," she repeated.

"There isn't 'maybe just sometimes,'" he said. "You need to think that 'maybe just sometimes' won't work. 'Maybe just sometimes' isn't a good answer.

"You're either a little well-trained little whore or

not."

And she got her butt smacked again. Harder than before.

Helen was kept in Frank's loft—locked in, hour after hour, day after day. No TV, no books, no radio, no magazines, no windows. Nothing. She thought to ask him to bring books or a small TV or *something*, but decided he probably wouldn't bother.

She began to imagine scenarios—for him, before he thought of any himself. She didn't have anything to write them down—no notepad—she hunted for paper and a pencil or a pen and found nothing.

Frank had locked away her clothes—she usually wore only panties.

So she remembered the scenarios and acted them out, Before he could think of nastier ones himself. As many as she thought possible. And they usually ended up with her pinned under him, getting fucked.

One Day—

She heard the lock in the door. "Hi honey," she chirped like a young bride. "I'm so glad you're home."

He walked in, without greeting her, Opened the refrig and popped the top of a beer can. She came to him, and pressed herself against him.

"Honey," she said, softly, " most of us girls are

so modest—there are things must girls can't say to men. They are, well—hard to say. But women need intimate things, feminine products.

"You know, We are so small in some places and so tight—well—we all need lubricants—oils, you know—even more vasoline. Oh dear, it's so hard to say this out loud—can you—would you—stop at a good store and get some—well, products for my little feminine parts?

"Girls lubricate themselves privately—and modestly—but some of them let their men watch.

"Oh, it's just too hard to say—I'm just such a modest girl (never mind she was only wearing panties in front of him).

"I have kind of forgotten names of some of them lubricants—oils—even baby oil would help. It's not expensive. Al girls need them for their little girl areas—

"Please—

"Some men make love to their little girls nice and gently—but some men don't—some never do—"

She wiped her pussy with plenty of vasoline, with three fingers, as he watched, drinking the beer.

He carried her to the bed, then, and fucked her as deeply as usual, pinning her down, with her ankles on his shoulders, and her butt tipped up.

But he did bring her a couple of bottles of feminine lubricants. And a small bottle of baby oil. Cheap ones, she noticed. (*Can you get these things at those dollar stores?* she thought.)

Another Day—

"Honey," said in her modest bride voice, "do you know how much oil could be poured into a girl? Into her—well, into her—private parts?

"A squeeze bottle—a plastic picnic ketchup bottle from a dollar store—with a small pour tube—filled with baby oil—and if the girl was put in a position—flat on a bed, with her legs up and her butt facing straight up—raised on a pillow or such—and her feet pointing toward the ceiling—a squeeze bottle of baby oil—

"The neck could be inserted slowly—into her—well, what do some people call it? Into her pussy? How much of the oil could she take? Some of the bottle? A half bottle of baby oil? More?

"If a tarp was put on the bed, then if she was lying on the tarp—things could get messy. The man could put his big thing into her to see how much of the oil could be squeezed out, while he was in her.

"Don't you think?"

He did get a tarp and a squeeze bottle—larger than she thought they made—at least larger than picnic ketchup bottle—probably from a dollar store—and baby oil. She lay on the tarp, on her back, he stuffed a pillow under her butt and told her to keep her legs raised toward the ceiling. And of course, spread apart. He inserted the plastic bottle pour spout into her pussy. She felt a warm liquid flowing into her.

He told her—over half of the bottle had slowly flowed into her—He kept her legs up, she felt some trickle down her belly and drip onto the tarp.

He kept her legs up and apart and entered her then—she felt the oil squeeze out as he thrust and thrust. It *was* messy—as she expected. Messy. Baby oil oozed out and flowed onto her belly and onto the tarp. He fucked her while holding her legs up. He came finally, adding his cum to the mess.He let her go. They felt to the tarp.

"Messy bitch," he said.

She wiped herself clean, but baby oil slowly oozed out of her for hours.

Another Day—

When she heard his key in the door, she had a beer popped open for him.

"How much," she said, wearing red panties only, "If a girl was put on her back, her ankles on a man's shoulders—how deep—how deep into her little pussy—do you think he could go?

"Could he make her little pussy ever deeper than it was, as an adult woman?"

He put her on the bed then, flat on her back. She pulled her legs up to her chest without him telling her, to put her ankles on his shoulders. Her butt tipped up, He entered her then, and lowered himself on to her. She felt trapped again. Her upraised butt an invitation to fuck her pussy—it made her gasp.

Then he thrust, again and again and again and again—she moaned slightly with every thrust, *ooohhh, oooohhh ooohhh, again and again.*

"You want a deeper pussy?" His mouth was close to her left ear.

"Go ahead and try."

His fucking seemed to take a long time.

Every thrust slow, powerful.

It was terribly intense for her.

He finally came in her. And slowly pulled out. Her legs fell from his shoulders.

"I'll be sore from that," she said.

"You'll be kept sore," he said.

Another Day—

When he came in, she was pacing back and forth, wearing just her black panties.

He looked at her curiously.

"If you keep an animal in a cage—even if it is in a big cage—it'll go into heat eventually, in the cage."

She continued to pace back and forth.

"In a cage, in heat. All female animals come into heat.

"They should be bred then, you know? They

may not want it—but they should be bred when they are in heat. They—large animals—are always frantic in heat."

He left the room, She heard the door lock and when he came, he held coils of rope. Heavier than clothesline rope—a outdoor hemp-type rope. She kept pacing, but he caught her. He held her arms behind her back and began wrapping it around her arms. Above the elbows. He didn't bother to tie her wrists,—the rope kept her arms behind her back. It seemed to take a long time.

"Bitch in heat," she said and shook her shoulders so her breasts swayed.

He smacked her butt then.

He held the ropes with one hand and smacked her again.

"Get you little butt bright red. And burning."

She got smacked again and again. She began to feel her behind getting warm. And warmer each time he hit her.

Then she didn't know when he was going to stop. It made her frantic.

And more. She didn't count, but maybe 12 times.

He pulled her down to her knees and held the back of her head.

He put his cock in her mouth and then held her head with both hands.

He thrust and thrust, deliberately trying to completely fill her mouth. She moaned with her mouth full.

She gagged on his cock and then again. And again. She felt drool slip down her chin. There was nothing she could possibly do to prevent him from raping her mouth.

He came finally, shooting his hot cum into the back of her mouth.

"Swallow it."

She gagged again and tried to swallow. He pulled out of her mouth and cleaned his cock by wiping it on each side of her face.

He pulled her to the bed and threw her face down.

"Stay there."

And then he pulled her legs apart. "*Stay like that. Don't move.*"

She spent the rest of the day face down on the bed with her arms bound behind her. Occasionally when she least expected it, he came over and spanked her butt again.

Those were the only scenes she could remember without writing them down somewhere.

Eventually the jar of vasoline he gave her was completely used up. Empty.

"Honey," she said in her modest bride's voice, "I do need some more—well, feminine products. It' sso hard to say—I am such a virgin bride—something

in the intimate products aisle in a store. Do please—
(She was wearing only white low-cut panties at the time she was describing herself as a modest little virginal girl.)

"It's so embarrassing to say what a girl needs. For her private parts—"

He brought back another jar of a generic vasoline, probably from a dollar store, or some Walmart type-store, but larger than the first.

"Don't lose it."

She knew exactly what she was saying, but couldn't resist saying it anyway.

"Don't lose it? Where would I lose it? I'm always locked up—I'm in a cage. I'm almost naked. I just wear a pair of panties every day."

She held the jar in the palm of her right hand.

"Where would I lose this? Could I hide it inside my panties?"

She then got a spanking. And for a few days after that, day after day, to keep her butt sore, she got spanked again. And again. And again.

Every time he began to spank her, she said the same thing—it was some defiance, but mostly humiliation.

"I'm kept almost naked. I'm locked in here. Where can I hide a jar of vasoline? Where in this one room can I lose it?

"Where can I hide it? I always just have a pair of panties on—" and *"you fuck me any time you want*

it—" and *"I suck you any time you want it—"*

She didn't know how many times he'd spank her.

Sometimes thought her behind would never feel normal again.

"Here," he said, one afternoon, giving her something in a package. "Put on your push-up bra first."

She put on the bra, then opened the package

A denim vest, It fit perfectly and was the right size.

The bra fit perfectly under her vest; on the back of the vest was the snarling panther and *Los Gatos*, toward the top and *Oakland* at the bottom.

"If you're going to be a biker bitch, you ought to look like one—"

She wore the bra and vest the rest of the night.

Frank seemed to like her with it on. The bra certainly felt different than those she was used to. The top of her breasts were so exposed, so lifted up, so *on display* for him.

She loved the vest, with the black panther on the back.

"Thank you Frank," she said, when they were going to bed and she meant it. She wore the bra and the vest, but nothing else. She knew he'd want to fuck her and she wanted to be screwed, to be totally fucked.

He pulled her ankles onto his shoulders, and fucked her as deeply as he could, thrust after thrust and before coming, let her legs down, so she could squirm under him.

She thought he was going to come on top of her, but he pulled out and she eagerly swung down and began sucking him. He came in her mouth and she swallowed it avidly, and then came herself, waves of climaxes, one after one. She went to sleep wearing her bra and denim vest, curled up, warm, between his legs, the taste of his semen in her mouth and the smell of him in her cocoon under the covers.

The lease ran out on Helen's San Francisco place—and since she was living with Frank, there was little need to keep paying for a place she no longer needed. She wrote to her younger sister Kathy, who lived with her own boyfriend in San Jose, and asked Kathy to clean out the place; she sent Kathy the key and told her she would write soon.

A few days later, during an afternoon ride, Frank stooped at a gas station to go to the john. Helen called her sister. Kathy had taken all Helen's things out of place and given the key to the manager. It was all settled. Helen told Frank that everything was out of her place and her sister closed the lease. There was no going back; she was living with Frank now and she had no place to go *to* except to her sister's and then only for a visit.

Frank was so pleased he said he wanted to give her a gift—and now. She wondered what it would be. Frank drove to a suburban shopping center. It seemed to her that she hadn't been shopping for *years*. They walked through the busy shopping mall.

Even with his chopper parked outside, they both received a number of stares. Frank wore his *colors*, the vest with the snarling panther on the back and *Los Gatos* and *Oakland* on the top and bottom. Frank was a hard-core biker and she was now his biker bitch—the straights of the world stared at her too. Well, she didn't mind. Frank was her man and she was proud of him.

Frank took her to a small shop in a corner of the shopping center, "The Piercing Palace." It was little more than a booth. A brassy blonde stood behind the counter. The counter windows were full of ear-rings, gold and silver. Helen didn't wear ear-rings—they didn't match well with her complexion and look and clothes.

"I want you to get your ears pierced. Today," Frank said.

She gasped. "But it'll hurt—Frank—I—"

The blonde behind the counter patted her on the back of her hand.

"Nothing to it, honey. Girls have it done all the time. We have some aerosol spray that numbs your ears then we quickly pierce them and you wear a set of training studs which are specially designed to prevent infection, then after a few days, you can wear whatever ear-rings you like. Or your man likes."

The blonde was about 45 and wore too much makeup. Helen didn't like her. She wore a pair of dangling gold ear-rings.

"But Frank—please—I'm glad for a gift, but—"

He was adamant. "Now. Right now. It won't hurt at all—she's right."

So Helen sat behind the counter. She hoped it wouldn't hurt. The woman washed her hands, put on surgical gloves and sprayed her ears with some sort of spray that felt chillingly cold. Helen felt the woman's hands on her ears—Helen couldn't feel much—after the spray. The woman's hands were busy; Helen was glad there wasn't a mirror in front of her. She didn't want to watch.

The woman walked behind Helen, spayed her right earlobe and continued. Helen again felt nothing. She *was* glad the procedure was painless. She felt something slightly heavy in her ear-lobe. Then again in her left ear lobe. The woman held up a mirror. Helen had gold studs through each ear-lobe, which screwed together from the back. "There, nothing to it, honey."

Helen couldn't see clearly. But there hadn't been anything to it—and if it pleased Frank—the studs weren't very heavy.

"Frank—I—" She got up. She turned to him.

"I have to go to the bathroom. It made me have to pee—"

"Go ahead."

The woman behind the counter gave her directions. She didn't realize that long ride in the cold earlier behind Frank on his chopper and the piercing would make her pee so urgently.

"I'll buy some ear-rings when you can wear a regular set," he said. Helen practically ran to the women's room in the mall.

They returned to the loft without incident. Helen again looked at herself in the mirror. Gold ear-studs against her blonde hair wasn't so bad, she thought. She did feel a slight difference—a slight weight pulling at her ears. But in a day or two, the weight became normal for her and she soon forgot about them.

It seemed to her that Frank fucked her every night. He hardly ever missed a night. Every night he took her—almost but not quite raping her, then forced her head down when he felt his climax coming, and she had to take his hard cock in her mouth, sucking him until he came. He always held her head down.

She never, ever, quite got used to it—especially since she never quite knew when his hot semen would spurt into her mouth. It seemed to her that he spurted his cum more and more each night. She once had a daydream that some night he would just cum and cum, without stopping, buckets of come, spurting and spurting into her mouth, faster than she could swallow.

At least she thought he might do that much.

Once, as he was climaxing, holding her head tight against his groin, her nose in his pubic hair, she tried to get up. She didn't care for this—at least this night. But he held her head firmly and spurted his hot cum into her mouth. She had to swallow. And swallow. And, as usual, he didn't let he get up to go wash out her mouth. She had to sleep curled between his legs, all night. She didn't get a chance to wash out her mouth until the next morning.

He looked down at her.

"From now on, you sleep with your mouth full. All night," He as holding up the covers so he could see her face.

"All night, Helen. If I wake up and my cock isn't in your mouth, I'll hang you by the pulleys and whip you all morning. Remember the rope you thought would split your little pussy in two? That's nothing—from now on—put it in your mouth—NOW—and stay that way. Or you're get punished the next morning."

"But Frank—" She was desperate—she knew she couldn't sleep like that. "I'll fall asleep. I can't—you wouldn't get any sleep. All night? Please—"

"I'll sleep fine. You can lie sideways with your

head on one of my upper legs.. Don't worry about your head on my leg. Put it back in your mouth."

He raised one leg so she could curl up, with her head resting on the top of his thigh. He watched as she put his semi-erect cock back into her mouth.

"All the way."

She took his cock until her nose was buried in his public hair. Then he slowly dropped his other leg over her own legs.

"Remember, if I awake up and my cock isn't in your mouth, you'll get whipped the next morning. Every night, bitch. Starting now. Alright?"

She had him in her mouth and could feel him slowly getting erect again.

"Alright?"

She nodded slightly.

"*MMMMMMM.*"

"Remember it," and he dropped the covers over her and slowly went to sleep. She had a harder time. She tried to stay awake, nursing his cock like a baby nursing a bottle. She finally dozed off with her left arm over his legs. She awoke once and his cock had slipped out of her mouth. She carefully picked it up— it was now completely soft—and put it back in her mouth. She didn't want him to wake up and discover she had fallen asleep let it slip from her mouth. He hadn't noticed.

She finally felt him stir. She hadn't slept well, but she *had* concentrated on keeping his thing in her mouth. To keep from getting a whipping, her arms pulled over her head, hanging from the pulleys.

She felt the covers being pulled back.

"You look good pussy. You did alright."

Morning. It must be morning.

"I didn't sleep well, Frank. I can't do this every night."

"You'll get used to it. In a few weeks, you'll think it's the most natural thing in the world to sleep with your man's cock in your mouth. You'll learn to sleep like a baby. Sooner or later, you'll ask for it. Every night. It won't feel right to go to sleep without being curled up and your man's thing in your mouth—"

She felt a warm wave of humiliation flow through her.

"But Frank—"

"Say thank you." He held her chin up with the palm of one hand.

"Frank—I—"

"Say thank you to it."

"She looked down. It seemed to be getting hard again.

She gave it a kiss.

"Thank you," she said to his cock.

"Remember Helen, every night. Soon you'll think it's the best thing in the world to go to sleep with your man's thing in your mouth. You'll remember all day what it feels like to go to sleep and wake up with my thing in your mouth. All nice and wet. Won't you?"

She felt another warm wave of humiliation flow through her.

"Yes, Frank," she said. And she didn't forget. All day. She thought of what it was like to lie all night with his cock nestled in her mouth. He was right. She didn't forget what that was like. But she wondered if she could ever get used to it.

One Friday night they were in the Roamin' Eye, at the bar, drinking beer when one of Frank's friends came up, a huge biker with the nickname Slick on the top left front of his biker vest.

"Who's your new chick, Frank? You never introduced her to everyone—"

Frank looked at him. Helen looked around. There must be about 40 bikers in the bar, some with women, some not. Drinking, shooting, pool—she hadn't ever seen so many in the bar at the same time.

Frank climbed onto the bar.

"Want you to meet my new chick." He had to shout to be heard above the usual din.

"This is Helen—" Frank reached down and pulled her onto a barstool. She used to work in San Francisco. She went to college before that. She loves choppers and bikers. She's livin' with me. Say hello to Helen—";

She waved tentatively to the crowd.

One of the bikers yelled—"That's no outfit a for

a biker's woman—lets' see some ass in those levis—"

Another yelled. "Cut-offs—she needs cut-offs—"

Then several were yelling. One just pushed his woman toward the bar. "Lois will fix up those jeans so she looks like a real biker bitch—"

Helen climbed down from the barstool. The woman named Lois looked at her.

"Turn around—" Helen turned around. "Designer jeans—nope. Babe, you need something that the all guys will like—"

Lois wore old levis, cut short, short, and a vest with her name on it.

Lois bent over and spoke something softly to the bartender.

Frank had climbed down from the bar and stood watching them. Lois took something from the bartender.

"Pool cue chalk," she said. "It'll be good enough to mark those jeans with. Legs apart honey." Lois began marking on the back of Helen's designer jeans with the chalk. Frank watched. Helen felt the chalk over the cheeks of her behind.

"Scissors," Lois told the bartender. He gave a her a pair of scissors from behind the bar.

"Come on, we'll do the rest in the women's room." Lois escorted her to the women's room, a dingy room toward the farther end of the Roamin' Eye.

"Take off your jeans," she said. Lois pierced them with the point of the scissors and began to cut, following the chalk lines she had drawn on the jeans.

"You'll have to take off your panties, honey—these are cut too high—they'll make your panties show—"

Helen was wearing her white panties, with the slight v-cut in the top front and back.

Helen felt another warm wave of humiliation. But she entered one of the stalls and took off her panties. She felt a second wave of humiliation flow through her, as she waited, naked from her waist to her boots, wearing nothing but her boots, bra and biker vest.

Lois reached through the unlocked stall door and held out a hand.

Helen absentmindedly gave the woman her the white panties.

"Here," Lois said, "Try these on—these are the way the guys like to see their women."

Helen took the jeans. There was barely anything left of them—she pulled them on. The jeans had been cut so high that the bottom half of her behind—her cheeks were fully exposed. There was barely anything in the front either. The material curved down into the cleft of—her pussy, barely keeping it covered.

"I'll give your panties to Frank," Lois said.

Helen walked back to the bar. She felt another wave of humiliation she was almost completely exposed from her waist to her boots. She felt the cool of the bar's air conditioning system on bare bottom.

Frank surveyed her.

"That's better." He climbed onto the bar.

"Here she is again—like her better this time?"

He held out his hands and she climbed onto the bar. There was a chorus of obscene shouts.

She felt that every in the bar was on her nearly bare behind. Frank turned her around so everyone could see that how her designer jeans had been cut so the bottom half of her cheeks showed completely— Lois had been right—she could have never worn a pair of panties—they could be seen, the jeans were cut off so high. The chorus of lewd comments continued. Helen didn't know what to do or say.

Lois climbed onto the bar.

"Here Frank, she wants you to have then—she doesn't need them." Lois waved Helen's panties, then gave them to Frank. There was another chorus of jeering and obscene comments.

Helen climbed down. Frank jumped off the bar. Lois had disappeared into the crowd. "Oh Frank—no everyone knows I'm not wearing anything under my jeans—"

He turned slowly toward her.

"Shows off your ass and your legs—and all—I think you ought to dress like this more often. Starting now. If you have any other pair of those designer jeans, we'll cut the others down too. From now on. Don't forget. You don't need those ritzy jeans. Look—
"

Helen saw that several of the other biker women wore cutoffs in the same way—exposing most of their asses and worn so tightly that she could see the cleft of their pussies.

"Frank—I—" she felt herself redden again. Everyone had seen her. Almost all of her behind. And they all knew that she had nothing under her cutoffs. Lois had seen to that—by giving Frank her panties in front of everyone.

"But Frank—I—" she began again.

He took her by the nape of her neck.

"Not another word. Don't you bitch at all. Not another word!" He turned and began talking to one of his biker buddies. She felt totally exposed, wearing almost nothing from her boots to her waist. She zipped up her biker jacket, but still felt exposed.

When they got back to the loft, he gave her three rules. To *always* remember. *ALWAYS REMEMBER*:

She'll always wear the smallest cutoffs in public, showing off her half-naked butt.

She'll never sit down at the bar or anywhere elsewhere—to cover up her butt—she'll always stand up.

She'd always stand with her legs spread apart.

In the Bar—

One weekend night, Frank and Helen in the

Roamin' Eye bar—Frank half sitting on a barstool, half leaning on the bar, turned sideways watching the crowd. Helen, beside him, in her push-up bra, biker vest, cutoffs and white knee-length boots. She standing, feet apart, at the bar, both forearms on the bar. Each holding a bottle of beer. He watching the crowd, she facing the bar.

A biker approached, on her side. Greasy levis— dirty t-shirt, biker vest with the Harley emblem where most had their names.

He approached on Helen's side.

"Frank—gonna get some of that tonight?"

Frank saw and nudged to Helen: *you reply.*

She turned toward the biker.She had a flashback to her taunt to Frank, earlier, much earlier.

Got any dark chocolate pussy nearby?

She tipped the beer bottle up, took a drink and looked directly at the biker.

"He gets pussy any time he wants it—" She took another drink from her beer.

"And any way he wants it—"

She paused.

"*Almost* any way he wants it—"

She tipped the bottle up again.

"*Almost* any way he wants it—" she repeated.

"The pussy is always sore, but he hasn't damaged it yet—"

She looked directly at the biker.

"Bitch's mouth is always sore. Used a lot. He says

hard to tell which is better—soft wet pussy or soft wet mouth.

"The bitch's favorite perfume is always his come on her face—"

She turned away from the biker, facing away from him.

"Enjoy the view—" she said, knowing her nearly naked butt was facing him.

"Damn!" she heard him say as he disappeared in the crowd.

She looked directly at Frank.

"Your little bitch needs another beer—" and

"You gonna want some pussy tonight?"

In the Bar—

Frank and Helen again in the bar—he watching the crowd, she facing the bar, her legs apart, with her cutoffs showing her nearly butt to the bikers.

One other biker came up to Frank. He as about four inches taller and heavier, but seemed to defer to Frank. This one had J.C. on the left front of his denim vest.

"Frank, you're new ol' lady ought to meet Honey—whaddya think?"

"Could be," Frank said.

"The two of them ought to hang around together for a while, know what I mean?"

"Yeah, OK."

Helen didn't have the slightest idea what they were talking about.

"How about tomorrow, Frank? I'll bring Honey over around noon."

"OK."

The biker disappeared into the crowd. Helen didn't know what to think. They left finally and on the ride back to Frank's loft, Helen got terribly cold. She wished her designer jeans hadn't been trimmed into the shortest possible cutoffs. The night rides were usually fun, but her legs were freezing by the time they got back.

When they got to the loft, she took off her biker jacket and pulled off the cutoffs—what there was left of them. There was practically nothing to take off. She had a pair of bikini panties which were larger than her now cut-up jeans.

Frank gave her a smack on her bare ass.

"Get in bed."

She took off her denim vest and push-up bra and climbed into their bed. He didn't even want her pussy—he guided her onto her elbows and belly and slipped his cock into her mouth. He made her stroke it and lick it until he came. Then he simply pulled the sheets and covers over her. Then pulled them down again.

"Remember, bitch? In your mouth. All night. Just like I said. You'll grow to love it—won't be any way you'll get to sleep except if my cock is in your mouth—"

She took it out briefly. "Proud of your old lady tonight? Did all the bikers like my bare ass?"

He looked down at her. "You bet, bitch."

"Goodnight Frank," she said without looking at him. She kissed his cock and put it in her mouth and curled around his legs. He pushed her head down with one hand until her nose was in his public hair and belly.

He pulled the covers up over her.

"OK, bitch?"

"mmmmmMMMMM.mmmmHHHHHHHH," she mumbled with his thing in her mouth. Frank squeezed her once with his legs, then relaxed. He quickly went to sleep. Helen could only doze off and on all night, his thing constantly in her mouth.

Helen was sitting crossed-legged on the floor the next morning, wearing her cutoffs (they were comfortable inside, although too cold on chopper rides). She wore a t-shirt that read *Harley Riders Do It In The Dirt*. She was re-reading and old biker magazine which Frank had left on the floor. She had read the few magazines he had so many times that she had practically memorized them.

Frank had locked the rest of her clothes in the old streamer trunk, locked where she couldn't get at them.

He was downstairs working in his chopper shop. She heard steps on the stairs and the door being unlocked. Frank and the biker she had seen talking to Frank the night before. J.C. And a girl. That must be Honey, his girl.

Honey wore the same cutoffs that Helen wore— she had a t-shirt that said *I'm In Heat* and a denim vest with the word Honey on the top left side. *She looks older than I am*, Helen thought *And bigger. I'm a 35 of so—she must be* at least a 38 C or D cup. Honey was about Helen's height and weight and had naturally curly blonde hair.

"Helen, Frank said, "this is Honey. Honey, meet Helen."

"Hi," Helen said, getting up from the floor.

J.C. turned to Honey. "Thought you two ought to meet. You two could have some fun together—"

"Today, J.C.? Now—?" Helen thought she saw a sudden look of panic in Honey's eyes.

"Now. Get undressed."

"J.C.—" Honey pleaded, but began pulling her boots off.

Frank turned to Helen. "You too."

She stood with her legs apart, defiant.

"Why, Frank?"

He grabbed her hair and twisted it viciously.

"Because I told you to. Now. Bitch."

Helen felt stabs of pain throughout her scalp. She didn't want to undress in front of this strange biker she didn't know and in front of this girl. She looked at Honey—Honey had taken her boots off, and her cutoffs and t-shirt and was standing naked beside J.C, watching Helen. Honey had a barely visible thatch of blonde pubic hair.

"Don't make me wait, Bitch," Frank said.

Helen saw if it was necessary for Honey, she would have to undress too. She pulled her t-shirt over her head and dropped it on the floor. She was braless. She slipped out of her cutoffs and kicked them across the floor with one foot.

Helen watched J.C. and Frank walk to the side of the room where the pulleys hung from the ceiling. Where Frank had bound her with so much rope he had nearly split her pussy in half, with a rope between her legs. She had never forgotten how her pussy felt with the rope deeply imbedded in it, her arms bound behind her back.

Frank let down one end of the rope; J.C. held *something* or *somethings* he had in his biker jacket.

"Honey, come here. Now—" J.C. ordered without turning to her.

Naked, Honey obediently walked over to J.C.

"Hold out your hands—"

"Please J.C. not today—"

But it was useless to protest, Helen saw. Honey reluctantly held out her wrists. J.C. cuffed her wrists with padded leather wrists cuffs, which were joined by 6 inches of chrome chain.

"You too, Helen, come over here—" This time Frank gave the order.

Helen reluctantly walked to where the three others were standing. J.C had given Frank another set of the linked handcuffs. Frank handcuffed Helen's wrists as J.C. had done to Honey.

"Kneel. Both of you."

Honey and Helen got down on their knees— Honey facing J.C., Helen facing slightly to Honey's left.

"Face together."

Helen moved to face Honey.

"Hold your arms up—" Honey obeyed first, Helen a second or so later.

J.C. fed the rope under the chrome chain connecting Honey's wrist cuffs, then through Helen's chain, and tied the end to the rope above. They were now roped together.

"Face together. Belly to belly."

J.C. pushed Honey toward Helen.

"Closer," J.C. said, pushing Honey almost on top of Helen.

Helen had never felt a naked woman against her before. Their hips met, their breasts flattered against each other slightly, their noses almost touched. Helen could smell a faint perfume smell on Honey and— was she sure?—a faint smell of semen.

"Get up." Both climbed to their feet.

J.C. and Frank began pulling the slack out of the

rope. Their handcuffed wrists were pulled higher and higher until the girls were forced to stand on their tiptoes, facing each other. Their breasts were flattered against each other, their hips touching, their knees touched and Helen had to lean slightly sideways so they didn't bump noses.

Helen looked up. The rope was pulled tight and through the pulley wheel hung from the ceiling. The other end of the rope angled down—tightly, to where Frank held it. When Honey and Helen were hung from the ceiling so just their toes touched the floor, Frank lashed the other end of the rope to a ring set in a side wall.

He got a wide leather belt from the bottom of the trunk where he had locked Helen's clothes. He slipped it around both of them and buckled it at their waist level so there was just a slight amount of play in the belt.

"Don't want you two to get too uncomfortable," he said. Honey and Helen said nothing—they were too preoccupied trying to stand on tiptoe, without mashing their breasts together, or banging knees or bumping noses.

"We have to work for a while—" J.C. said, "My chopper needs some work. Get to know each other, girls, we'll play later."

Frank and J.C. walked to the door. Helen heard the door lock from the other side and their footsteps getting faint as they went downstairs.

"How you feelin'?" Helen said.

"OK, but I don't know how long I can stand like this. My arms hurt terribly." Helen's nose was against the side of Honey's head. They could speak softly into each other's ears.

"I don't know either," Helen said, "Let's try something. If I slide sideways a bit, I can fit one leg between your legs and maybe it'll be more comfortable—" (Helen didn't know how to talk to a naked woman—whether to say breasts or tits, or jugs or—or what?—vagina or pussy, or beaver, or snatch, or any one of the dozens of names men call it—vagina seemed too formal—but she did like the newest name—*the va-jayjay*—it sounded cute and was probably thought up by a woman.)

Helen tried slipping sideways three times until she succeeded. The two of then swung back and forth slightly, then Helen was able to slide one of her legs between Honey's legs. Helen's left breast lay snugly between Honey's larger breasts. Helen felt a slight patch of Honey's public hair.

They fit together better that way—with Helen's leg between both of Honey's legs and one of Helen's breasts nestled between Honey's bigger breasts. That position allowed slightly more slack in the belt around their waists.

"J.C. does this to me all the time well—seems like all the time—" Honey said, suddenly. "He gets a real kick out of seeing me hang like this. His place has a pulley like this—he loves to let me hang for a while until I get so sore and achey I'll do anything he wants me to. If only he'll let me down. I never know how long he makes me stand like this—with other girls—Eventually I'll do anything, anything, just to be let down."

Helen didn't quite know what to say.

"How long have you been with J.C?" It sounded like meaningless small talk, but it might take Honey's mind off being hung like this.

Honey told Helen her story. Honey had left a broken home at 15, and roamed around the streets of Berkeley for several years, sleeping here and sleeping there, getting by this way and that. Selling dope, dancing in a topless bar. Until she met J.C. by accident at an all-night diner.

She had been living with him for seven months. It was OK—she said—J.C. was good to her but he had this streak—he loved to make her obey. She never knew what she might have done to make him unhappy.

She tried her best to please him, she said, she *did* care for him—but on a regular basis—he'd tie her up like this—or in other ways—or whip her with a crop. He said he likes to see her butt marked.

"He does that—on a regular basis—I suspect I'll get a whipping soon—he whips me until my butt is crisscrossed with red welts, then he lets me heal— then whips me again. I can't sit down comfortably for a week or so—it takes that long or the welts to heal—then I'll know I'll get whipped again—" Honey paused for a moment.

"Between the whippings, he likes to watch me with another girl Usually one of the other biker girls. He likes to make me 'perform' as he says. Well, that's not so bad. I guess he'll want me to do you, Helen—" she paused again, trying to take a deep breathe. "Have you ever made it with another girl?"

"No," said Helen, talking into Honey's ear.

"It's not so bad—If he keeps me like this much longer, I'll plead with him to let me down. I may have to go down on you. I hope you won't mind. It doesn't hurt at all and it's more fun sometimes than makin' it with the guys—" Honey paused again as both of them tried be as comfortable as they could, hanging together on their tip—toes from the ceiling.

"I'll have to tell you—if he comes back and whips me with a crop-like whip—like he sometimes does— if he whips me long enough, I suddenly just pee. I can't help it. It hurts too much and I can't control it. I just pee. If he whips me today, like this—I may pee—I—"

"It's OK," Helen said. "It's OK." She wanted to say something else to Honey, but she didn't quite know how to respond to that.

"You been Frank's girl for very long?" Honey asked, and Helen told Honey her story—how she went to college, was bored, graduated, got a job in

San Francisco, never met a man who interested her or excited her. How she went to the Roamin' Eye for excitement one night, how she met Frank, how they eventually go to know one another, how she moved in with Frank. And how Frank telephoned and told her boss that she had quit. And—since Honey told her about being whipped—Helen told her how Frank made her sleep. Curled up between his legs. (Actually he slept on his side and she slept on her side, facing him, her face in his pubic hair and groin.) And how he made her sleep with his thing in her mouth all night long. And how she didn't sleep well like that, but she made sure that his thing was in her mouth all night long so she wouldn't get punished.

"God," Honey said, "I hope J.C. never thinks of that. I hope Frank never brags about that. I'll have to do that too. J.C. would love that. I hope he never finds out about that—"

"Well," Helen said, as they did an awkward dance on their toes, "Frank told me that eventually I'd get used to it—I wouldn't feel comfortable without having his thing in my mouth when I went to sleep. Don't *you* tell him, but I *do* find it comfortable. I'd never *dare* tell him that, but it *is* fun. I do feel comfortable unless it is in my mouth. I'd never dare tell him that. But it is fun. I do feel uncomfortable unless it *is* in my mouth. I just nurse it all night long, like a baby sucking on a bottle of milk. I *do* like it, although I could never tell him—"

Helen paused. She didn't know what else to say to Honey.

"You OK?" Honey asked. "Yeah," Helen aid, into Honey's ear. "OK, but my arms ache terribly."

"You feel nice," Honey said, It's nice and warm, having you like this. I like you between my tits, you know? Is that terrible?"

Helen smiled but knew Honey couldn't see her.

"No," she replied, "it's not terrible. I like my leg between yours—"

"You know," Honey said, "if the guys weren't here and we weren't hung up like this, it'd be fun just to put on warm nighties and just curl up together. You know? Not making it or anything. Just curled up and be warm. With your titties between mine and one of your legs between mine. Wouldn't that be nice?"

"Yes," Helen said, honestly, "I'd like that. (She never thought that she would say something like that about being with another girl, but it did sound nice and warm—)

"If J.C., comes back and whips me," Honey said, changing the subject abruptly, "I'll have to cry or scream. I hope I'm not too loud—like this—too close to your ears—"

"Nothing you can do about it—" Helen said, "Frank might whip me then I'll cry or scream in your ears—"

"Maybe both of them will want to whip both of us at the same time—" Honeys aid, "when one of the other bikers gets a good idea about something with his ol' lady—they pass things on. They may want to see which of us can scream the loudest, or take the most cuts with a crop or something—"

"Well, if you have to scream, go ahead," Helen said "and if I have to, I will—"

They were both silent for a moment or two,

"I have to go to the bathroom," Honey said, suddenly.

"Well, don't say anything about it—or they won't let you down. And don't say anything about it now, or I'll have to go too. I wonder how long we have been here?"

"Don't know, but it seems forever," Helen said.

They heard the sounds of a motorcycle engine revving downstairs in the shop.

"Must have gotten J.C.'s chopper fixed," Honey said. "We didn't know if we could get here or not, it was running so rough—"

They heard footsteps on the stairs, then J.C. and Frank unlocked the door and became back. Frank was wiping his hands on a shop rag.

"You two get acquainted?" J.C. asked.

"As well as we could," Honey said, "but it's not fun. Let me down, J.C./—" she pleaded.

"Maybe," J.C. said, "how good are you going to be?"

"Please, J.C.," Honey begged.

Helen couldn't see him; her back was to the

room; all she could see was the doorway to her right.

"Oh no—" she heard Honey cry, "no, J.C., please—"

"What?" Helen asked.

"He's got his crop now," Honey said, "I'm going to get a whipping—I'll have to cry—I guess—Helen—"

Helen felt herself being turned. Helen and Honey did a tiny dance on their toes, as Frank turned them so Helen was facing into the room and Honey's back and behind was presented to J.C.

"Please, J.C.—" Honey said, as she faced the wall and her back and behind was toward him. "Oh please, please don't—"

Helen could watch, her head was on the left side of Honey's; J.C. stood in front of Honey. Helen watched as J.C. flexed the crop once, twice.

She wanted to tell Honey that the first blow was coming, but she thought it might be easier if Honey didn't know when—she saw J.C. swing viciously. Honey howled with pain and both of them swung and danced toward the wall from the force of the bow.

He must have caught her toward the top of her butt, Helen thought.

J.C. swung again and again caught Honey's butt. Helen could hear the swwwwiiiissshhh the crop made in the air before it cut into Honey's behind. They both shook on the rope when Honey got whipped. Blow after blow; Helen wished she could check Honey's behind. It was probably deeply burning—Honey first yipped with the pain, the cried out, then howled when the crop bit into her behind.

J.C. was thorough—he whipped her butt, and calculated when to swing to get crisscross welts to appear.

Honey's cries were louder and louder, more insistent, more fearful.

Frank watched, behind J.C.

Wonder if he is learning how to whip a woman? Helen thought idly, *Or if he already knows. Or when he might want to try it on me.*

Honey thrashed more and more, *cried louder and louder.* She shook her head once and tears brushed Helen's cheeks.

"It's OK. It's OK," Helen tried to whisper—

"It'll be over soon—" she tried to whisper as softly as she could.

"You say something bitch?" J.C. asked her.

"No. No sir. Nothing," she said to J.C. She wondered if he would begin to whip her too—or—she wondered—if he would leave that to Frank. After all, she was Frank's woman, not his.

Honey moaned and cried, screamed then, when the crop bit into her. Helen thought she could see bits of blood fly from Honey's butt when the crop hit her, but she wasn't sure. She did know that Honey was being whipped hard and hard, often, and her screams were real. She was in great pain. And Helen could do nothing except feel Honey's breasts heave, and feel

Honey's legs kick when the crop forced her to do a dance on her tiptoes.

A warmth! A gushing inside Helen's thigh. Like Honey had said—she peed because of the pain. Peed down Helen's leg, which was nestled between Honey's legs. Helen felt the warm drip and stream down her upper thigh, from Honey's slit.

"It's OK—It's OK, Honey," Helen said. "Go ahead, it's OK."

"You want some too, bitch?" J.C. said to her.

"Frank," Helen called, "Are you going to let him whip me?"

Helen knew it was a challenge to Frank not to let J.C. whip her—even though there was a risk Frank might try to make her scream and cry as much as J.C. had done to Honey.

Or that Frank would let J.C. whip her.

"Please J.C.," Honey suddenly said, "I'll do anything. Just let me down. Don't whip me anymore. Please. *PLEASE*." There was more than a touch of panic in her voice.

"Tell me what—what—" J.C. asked, "what will you do now? If I let you down?"

"I'll—I'll do it with her if you want. If you want to watch—" Honey suddenly tried to whisper to Helen, "I'm sorry—"

"It'll be OK," Helen said. She didn't care how loud. She would talk to Honey if she wanted to and if Frank didn't like it, then he could whip her if he wanted to. Or he could probably let J.C. whip her.

"Want to watch Honey do your girl" J.C. said to Frank.

"Sure," he said, then turned and walked over and stood in front of Helen.

"Today's your turn for Honey to do you—your turn is next if you get bitchy again. Understand?"

J.C. let the two girls down. Helen was able to stand on her feet as Frank took the handcuffs off— Honey slipped to the floor. J.C. had to make her hold her hands up to his waist to get the cuffs off her wrists.

"Come on," J.C. said to Helen. He grabbed her by the elbow and escorted her to the bed. "Down," He turned toward Honey, still on the floor. "Come here and do her," Honey slowly crawled over to the bed and inched her way upon to it.

"Spread your legs, bitch," J.C. said to Helen. She opened her legs and hiked her knees slightly.

Honey crawled up the bed on her belly and smiled weakly at Helen, then wrapped her forearms around Helen's legs and buried her face in Helen's public thatch. She then felt Honey's tongue licking inside her slit, up and down her pussy. Helen's eyes were open—she saw Frank and J.C. standing over her.

The tongue inside Helen's slit continued to lick and probe—Helen felt herself warming. She reached down and curled her fingers into Honey's curly hair; Helen closed her eyes. Honey was *good*. Helen wondered how Honey could be so good and energetic after the whipping she had just received.

Helen looked down. She could see red welts cross-crossing Honey's behind.

Honey's tongue continued its work. Helen lay with her eyes closed.

"Crawl up and kiss her," J.C. suddenly said to Honey.

Helen felt the tongue stop—then her slit was empty.

She felt Honey's tits on top of hers—she opened her eyes.

"It's OK," Honey said, her face over Helen's.

"Open your mouth when I kiss you—they want to see us frenching each other."

Helen opened her mouth. She had been kissed on the cheek by other women—but never had a woman kiss her open mouth, like she had done with men.

She felt Honey's small tongue dart in and out of her mouth, felt Honey's tongue meet hers. Honey's fingers explored Helen's slit—Helen involuntarily wrapped her arms around Honey's back. Honey stiffened. "Sorry," she said. She had been too rough too close to where Honey had been whipped.

"Go back down" J.C. said to Honey," get her off."

Honey slid down and Helen again felt the tongue inside her slit, Honey's forearms again wrapped around Helen's legs. The tongue continued to lick and explore up and down inside Helen's pussy.

Helen felt herself get warmer and wetter, felt her hips buck against Honey's head. Then waves of warmth, from deep inside her. Helen let go and came and came. It was the first time she had come with a woman—that surprised her. She didn't think that she would have been able to climax when Honey licked her so. But she had. She had climaxed almost as well as she might have, with a man. With Frank.

Helen moaned and bucked and held Honey's head down, held Honey's face and tongue deep inside her thatch of public hair. She didn't want Honey's tongue to leave her slit. But the warmth was dying now, the waves of climax disappearing. Honey must have felt Helen's climax dying. The tongue slipped out of Helen's slit. Then she felt Honey on top of her again.

"OK?" Honey asked. She was on her elbows, looking down at Helen.

"Sure. OK. Fine. Thanks." Helen wrapped her arms around Honey's neck and gave her an open-mouth Kiss. She *was* thankful. Honey *was* super. It had felt so good. Helen was happy that Honey had gone down on her. She was sorry that Honey had been whipped, but happy that Honey's tongue had pleased her so. The kiss ended.

"Thanks Honey," she said again. "It was nice," she said softly.

"Come on bitch," she heard J,.C. say to Honey. "Shows over, Get dressed. I got other stuff to do."

Honey reluctantly got up and slowly dressed.

"See you again," Helen said softly to Honey.

"Hope so," Honey replied. She was dressed. J.C. smacked her hard on her butt. "Come on bitch." He pushed her through the door. Helen heard their footsteps going down the stairs, then she heard J.C.'s chopper—then they were gone.

Helen looked around. Frank had undressed. He was erect.

"My turn now," he said. He laid on his back on the bed and Helen lay on her belly, on her elbows and sucked him until he climaxed. She had to swallow it, as always, then both of them were exhausted. Franck had watched Honey and Helen bound and Honey whipped, then Helen was exhausted from being bound with Honey, then having Honey go down on her, then doing Frank.

They slept together the rest of the afternoon, Frank on his side, Helen under the covers, curled up, Frank's thing deeply in her mouth, one of his legs over hers. She woke now and then and slowly and softly sucked him, nursed his thing like a baby would suck on a bottle. She *did* like it. Just like he said she would. Now when they went to bed, she quickly and automatically put his thing in her mouth and curled up, her head on the inside of his thigh. And she slept all night, or woke then slept, his thing always in her mouth.

The next night, Frank took her on the back of his chopper into downtown Oakland. "It's time for you to get a job, babe," he said, before they started. They drove to a big topless place, "The Silver Dollar," Frank walked through the place as if he had been there before.

It was, as Helen once heard a college boy call them, a "titty bar."

There were two stages, with a girl dancing on each stage. Both girls wore nothing more than a g-string, high heels and a smile. Nothing much else. Pasties, Helen later saw. Not visible from a distance. She tailed along behind Frank. There was a DJ in a large booth, high over one stage. He put on CD selections for the girls to dance to. Frank walked through the club to an office behind the bar. He just walked in without knocking. Helen followed.

A huge man sat behind a desk. "Helen, this is Big Gil. Gil, this is Helen. My new chick." The man behind the desk didn't rise to shake her hand. He slowly lit a cigar.

"Turn around, babe."

Helen slowly turned around.

"Looks OK Frank."

"Got some things, babe?" Gil asked her.

Helen didn't know what to say.

"For what?"

He laughed. "Dancing. pasties, g-strings—that stuff—Frank signed you up to dance here—"

Helen looked at Frank

"I can't. Frank—you shouldn't—"

She balled her hands into fists. "I won't do it. I'm not a topless dancer—"

Frank grabbed her by her hair and smacked her hard on her butt.

"You've had a free ride long enough. Gil here is an old biker friend of mine. He offered you a job here. Can't you be courteous enough to take it? You're going to work from now on. Topless dancing isn't hard. There is nothing to it. Of course, you have to wait on tables and deliver drinks between your sets, but there's nothing easier—you'll get used to it in a few days—"

"No Frank, listen—I—"

"I'm leaving. Work something out with Gil. He offered you a job. I'll be back in a half hour or so. OK?"

"OK, Frank," Gil said. "We'll get together on something with your chick here." Frank left the office.

Helen didn't know where to start. "Gil, I've been with Frank only a few weeks—months—actually, and I—" She didn't know how to explain that she had been to college and had a good job in San Francisco—

"I've never been a dancer and I don't think I'd be a good—a topless dancer—a good dancer." She suddenly had an idea.

"Look, you probably need a new waitress just as well as dancers, Just let me be a waitress for a few days or a week or two and let me watch the dancers and make up my mind later. I really don't have any dance costumes anyhow. And if you'll give me a few weeks—"she shortened that to—" a few days at least to watch and pick up some pointers and then maybe I'll—I'll learn how and then—"

He leaned back so far that Helen thought he'd fall off his chair.

"Just as a favor to Frank. The money isn't as good as the dancers get. You can start as a waitress. A week or so, then you make up your mind. Two weeks tops. Frank'll be disappointed. All the dancers get top money. Most of them are biker women here. Nothing to it."

He dialed a number on his cellphone.

"Louise? Gill. I got a new girl as a waitress. Set her up with a costume and let me know how much. I'll pay for it and take it out of her first paycheck. Ok? Thanks."

He hung up. He scrawled the name of a lingerie shop on the back of a business card.

"Go on over tomorrow morning. Louise has all sizes. She'll fix you up with the type of costume most of our girls wear. The waitresses."

He relit his cigar, which had gone out.

"Remember. A week. Two weeks at most. Then you decide if you want to dance. Frank'll be unhappy. Dancers earn better money than waitresses. You be here at two p.m. tomorrow. Louise will have your costume ready tomorrow morning. OK? If I have anything else, I'll call Frank."

Helen walked out of the office and sat at the bar. She bought herself a beer and waited for Frank. She never thought that she would be living with a biker who would get her a job in a topless club. Even as a waitress. She remembered all the college courses she had taken—

—Frank returned. "All set, babe?" She didn't want to tell, him that she refused to be a topless dancer and had bargained with Gil to let her begin as a waitress.

Frank took her back to the city the next morning, to the lingerie shop.

There was a sign in the shop:

Naughty Things for Good Girls
Good Things for Naughty Girls
—Which Are You?

The woman, Louise, knew who she would be working for. Helen gave Louise her sizes: Louise rummaged through some boxes and shelves behind the counter.

"Here, these will all fit."

Helen tried on the outfit in a dressing room: black panties, an old-fashioned garter belt, fishnet stockings (she had never had a pair) and four-inch black high heels. A black satin skirt that barely covered the tops of her stockings, a white push-up bra and a white satin blouse with a deep V that showed her cleavage. "I'll send Gil the bill," Louise said.

Helen could hardly keep her high heels on the footpegs of Frank's chopper. She could hardly walk in the high heels. She hadn't worn spike heels in years. She couldn't remember the last time she had such a pair of heels.

Frank took her to the topless club, to Gil's office. "Looks good, babe." Gil turned to Frank. "Two to two—p.m. to a.m. If you want to pick her up, we'll be closing about 2:10." Frank nodded.

Helen was taught which section of the bar was hers, how not to get drink orders mixed up, where the waitresses area of the bar was, how to run the cash register if the bartender was busy. She had problems with her high heels. They made her feet sore, the toes were pointed so and the height made her totter and made her ankles hurt.

She learned to dread the work. The hours were brutal; twelve hours with only about 45 minutes for lunch about 8 p.m.

Once a night she could count on a customer reaching up under her skirt or slapping her butt or hustling her for a date. Her feat hurt constantly. She fell twice in the first week, when one ankle twisted. She didn't think she could ever get used the high heels. Or the outfit. *Makes me look like a tart*, she thought. She once asked one of the other waitresses why they all had to wear old-fashioned garter belts and hose.

"When we bend over, honey, the customers get to see a flash of your panties. That's a better thrill for them than if we just wore pantyhose. Don't you think? Sure, we look like hookers but aren't all women hookers in one way or another?" Helen didn't know what to say.

She didn't know how she survived the two weeks. At the end of the two weeks, she waited in Gil's office when the bar closed.

"What you need, babe?"

"My check."

Gil looked at her as if she was crazy.

"Most of it went to pay for your costume. We don't use paychecks here. Cash only. Ask Frank. I saw him when he dropped you off this morning. He stopped in here for a minute."

Frank! Frank took her pay. She said nothing to him the ride back to his loft. She pretended that everything was OK, that she was just tired after her twelve hours at work.

Inside the loft, Frank took off his biker jacket and threw it on the floor.

"Frank," she said, as innocently as possible, "Gil said he gave you pay—"

"Yeah, babe."

"Well?"

"Well, what?"

"Well, I want my pay. I worked *forever* for that."

Frank walked over to her and slapped her face.

"Don't even go any farther. You belong to me! You work when I say you work and stay home when I say stay home. That's the way it is. Gil gave me your pay,. All the biker women work there—all; their men work with Gil the same way,. Don't you get bitchy with me again. Not one more time."

"But Frank—"

He pulled her over to the bed and flipped her over his lap, held her head down, flipped her skirt up with his right hand, then awkwardly pulled her panties down toward her knees. She tried to kick and reach for him with her hands, but he held her hair so hard that her scalp ached. He padded her bare behind with his right hand. She felt her behind get red with the pain, sore, then achy. Frank continued to spank her. Blow after blow. She couldn't get up off lap. He twisted her hair back and forth and continued to spank her. She tried to protect her behind with her hands.

"Don't—" he commanded.

"Stop Frank. Stop, Stop PLEASE—"

"Don't you ever be bitchy with me. Not ever. Not ever again."

The blows continued on her bare behind. She remembered as a child when she was spanked once. It was nothing like this.

"Alright, Frank. Please. PLEASE."

He finally let her up. She was teary-eyed, her

behind burned, her scalp ached, her blouse was askew, her hair messed. She felt like crying

Frank looked at her, then began getting undressed.

"Come on," he said. She knew it, time for bed. Time to curl up between his legs and try to sleep with his thing in her mouth. All night. She took her blouse off and hung it on a chair. She took her bra off and dropped it on the same chair. Then pulled her skirt off, kicking her high heels off.

She walked over to the bed with her panties, garter-belt and hose on, then took them off beside the bed.

"Ok, Frank, OK." He was lying on his back, with his legs spread, waiting for her to curl up, as usual.

"But you're not getting any tonight. I really want to sleep now. Not try and stay awake sucking you all night. You can do without it tonight."

She was on her knees, naked, below him in the bed.

"Are you sure, babe? Absolutely sure of this?"

She curled up.

"Good night, Frank." She said, without looking at him.

"OK, babe," he said and pulled the covers up. For the first time in weeks she got a good nights sleep. Without sucking him,

She worked another week. Finally she couldn't stand it any more. She told Gil she wouldn't be back.

She said that she had worked things out with Frank. That they agreed that's she would work closer to his shop. She told Gil not to say anything to Frank—that she and Frank had discussed it. Gil shrugged.

"OK, kid," was all he said.

Frank picked her up a little after two a.m. as usual. He had gotten crankier and crankier during the week when she had gone to bed without sucking him. After weeks and weeks of getting some pussy or having her suck him, he now could do without it, she thought. A few days without any pussy would make him think again about her, she had thought. A few nights rest without his thing in her mouth all night would give her better rest and make him appreciate her.

She again simply curled up between his legs without taking him in her mouth.

"Good night, Frank," she said. And that was that.

He woke her the next morning. "Get up. You have to go to work—we have to be on the road in 45 minutes or so." "Not going, Frank," she said. "I told Gil that I wouldn't be back. You'll have to find something else for me to do. I told him that my feet were killing me in those high heels. I wouldn't be back. You called my old boss in San Francisco and told them I quit—remember? Now I told Gil—let me get some rest now—"

She lay on the bed, curled up, naked.

"You really are something," Frank said. "I thought you learned not to be bitchy. Thought that was all out of you. You'll have to learn a lesson you'll never forget—Come here—"

He stood at the edge of the bed. "Give me some head. You haven't sucked me for a week and a half—"

She looked up at him. "I'm really tired now, Frank. Maybe later—"

She wondered if he would beat her up.

"OK, babe," was all he said. He walked to the door, then left the loft, locking the door from the outside, as he left. She heard his steps on the stairs, going down to the chopper shop. She heard him disappeared on his chopper. She pulled the covers up to her shoulders and dozed off.

She woke up when she heard the key in the lock. Frank—was back. And J.C., the biker who had the girlfriend Honey. And two more. A small, dumpy-looking man, half bald, wearing a biker vest. And a small rat-faced guy—who looked like more of a kid than a real man.

"Time you learned a lesson, Helen. That you won't ever forget—" Before she could move, Frank yanked the covers from her and held her by her wrists. J.C. grabbed her legs. The third man helped Frank. The third held one wrist while Frank tied it tightly to the corner of the bed-frame. Then her other wrist—was tied. She saw the dumpy-looking man had a vest with the word DOC on it.

Then both of them helped J.C. with her legs. The two of them held one ankle and J.C. tied it to the bottom corner of the bed. Then the other ankle. She was securely spread-eagled to the bed, with the three bikers towering over her. Frank took a pair of her own panties—from yesterday—she could smell her own juices on them—and balled them up and stuffed them in her mouth, then taped over her mouth with duct tape. She looked at them wild-eyed with anxiety. She could feel her own heartbeat. She tried to twist her wrists but only succeeded in hurting herself.

Doc nodded to J.C.—who covered Helen's eyes with a cupped hand.

Doc had a small bag, took out a syringe, and gave her a quick injection in her upper arm.

He walked a couple steps toward Frank, and answered Franck's unspoken question.

"High dose of Demerol. It'll sedate her—she'll be almost out, but she'll just be able to know a little something of what is happening."

(Doc was—or had been—a real doctor, but got caught in a massive scheme to sell prescription drugs on the black market. Newspapers called it the biggest bust of that kind in recent state history. He plea-bargained his conviction to a few months in jail but lost his medical license.)

He had roamed around here and there, and finally joined the biker gang, not because he was a great biker—actually he drove an old pick-up truck, but because the gang protected him—he could still get all the drugs the bikers wanted and he could help them in times like this.

Helen would never know that the rat-faced kid was the most creative tattoo artist in Oakland. Frank hadn't known about him, but J.C. did—and recruited him for this job.

The four watched Helen—she seemed slowly to relax—like she was in a deep sleep.

"OK," Doc finally nodded.

He began to talk to her.

"Not going to hurt a bit, babe. Frank tells me you are too bitchy. Some of the other biker women have learned not to be bitchy. Just something today to help you behave. Didn't you say you didn't want Frank to have any more pussy for a while?

"Not going to hurt one little bit—" He sprayed her completely with a liquid from plastic bottle—she felt a deep cold, on her pussy, chest, all the way to her chin.

He paused, and sprayed her again—completely. And waited.

And sprayed her completely again. He turned to Frank and spoke softly.

"High level painkiller. She only feels cold—and numb."

He the loosened the ropes tying her ankles to the bed-frame, pulled her legs up slightly, doubled up a pillow and put it under her butt.

She heard a buzz. He was doing something near—her pussy—She tried and tried to understand what he was doing. She didn't know he was shaving her clean.

She felt the cold, and she was numb. She could nto see what he was doing to her—something. He was doing something. Her pussy was numb—the numbness reached into her thighs and up, up, up her chest and under her chin. Cold. And numb. He was doing *something* to her, but she couldn't see what and couldn't feel anything.

She tried to complain but could only manage a soft pleading—*MmMMMmmmm*—with her mouth stuffed with her own panties and taped with duct tape.

Frank and J.C. watched, fascinated. The rat-faced kid didn't seem to much care.

It took a while—Doc had to be very careful about exactly what he was doing. Doing to her—he had to know exactly how and where to work—he was, after all, a doctor, used to minor—well, minor surgical work. He wore surgical gloves—and everything he needed was surgically antiseptic. There would be no infections from any of his work.

He finally stepped back.

"Done now," he said, casually, toward Frank and J.C.

"You won't get any pussy from her from now on—"

Doc had pierced her—on both sides of her pussy lips and inserted a chrome ring. A bit higher than the middle of her pussy. It was big enough to take the shank of a padlock or the snap latch of a dog leash.

"It isn't near the outer edge of her pussylips—this is minor surgery—the piercing is as deep as I could get. Into her. The ring holds her pussy almost completely closed. You could get a little finger into her from the bottom of her pussy, but that's about all. She won't realize it at first—but she won't be able to pee easily. The only position she'll be able to pee is squatting down—say, over a shower drain, in a bathtub or squatting outside somewhere—

"And she also won't know—at first—that she can't use a tampon—can't get it into her for her periods. She'll need some of those adult—senior-citizen—diapers or she'll just have hold a towel between her legs. Your choice, Frank."

"But how—" Frank asked—

"The ring comes in two halves—one end of one half is the male end, with a small probe with a fishhook-type barb in it. The other end of the half circle looks to be empty, but slopes inward a bit—then there is a collar—or ridge. The probe with the fishhook barb slips into the empty end—male to female, male to female on each side—and once the fishhook barb passes the ridge inside the empty end—it can't be pulled out.

"And the ring is so tight into her, that there is no real way it can be cut apart once she is pierced. It would have to be surgically cut away from her or simply ripped out. Some damage to her there, with that idea.

Frank offered him two small items, held out in the palm of hand.

"We almost forgot—she'll need a new pair of ear-rings."

Doc took them from Frank, took out her training earring studs, inserted one of the new ear-rings what Frank had given him, clicked it closed, then clicked the second in place.

"She'll feel these are heavier—but she'll get used to them—soon."

Frank gave Doc the two small keys for the small padlocks.

"Souvenirs of the occasion for ya' Doc."

Time seemed to pass slowly for her. Or stop entirely. Once Doc asked, "numbness wearing off any?" She shook her head almost imperceptibly—a very small, very weak *NO*.

Then the rat-faced kid went to work. He had a template—a rough drawing on a kind of onion skin paper—he laid it on her chest, pressed down and got an outline.

He plugged in his tattoo pen and began.

If Helen had been really able to see well—all she would have seen was him bending over her chest. She would have felt the cold—cold, all over, from her pussy to her chin. But that would have been all. And she would have not been able to tell exactly what he was doing. But she couldn't focus well or attempt to understand what he was doing.

She heard some footsteps, but couldn't tell how much time had p[assed. Someone leaving the room? Or coming back? Whatever the rat-man was doing, it didn't seem hold the interest of the others. Was it minutes or hours? She heard the continuing buzz of some sort—and vaguely felt his hands on her, on her chest, up into her cleavage, now between her breasts, and up, over her left breast and down again. The buzzing. Then back to the breast itself, and, as far as she vaguely understood, toward her left nipple.

Then something else—suddenly he said "Tip your head back."

She couldn't comprehend what he meant.

He had to tip her head up, so she was staring at the ceiling.

Then the cold spray again. The coldness and the numbness of her chin and throat. Then the buzzing again. She vaguely felt his hands on her throat, holding her chin. Then done.

The buzzing stopped.

"OK," the rat-man said. "All done."

He packed up his gear—"I'll settle with you later," Frank said. The little rat-man just nodded and left.

Frank later paid him in drugs that Frank had, in turn, gotten from Doc.

Then they had to wait until the Demerol wore off. When she began to slowly move and look around Doc knew the sedation was dissipating. Frank slowly pulled the duck tape away from her mouth and took the balled-up panties out of her mouth.

She looked a little groggy, but she was back—awake.

"Get up," Frank said, and helped her up by holding one elbow. She was naked in front of three bikers. Frank led her to the bathroom door—the bathroom in the loft was just a half-bath—commode and sink. There was a factory-type shower downstairs, behind the parts area of the chopper shop. But there was a full-length mirror on the inside of the bathroom door.

Frank turned her toward the mirror.

"Look."

Helen turned and saw—

A tattoo! An enormous black panther had been tattooed on her belly and chest. One of the two men she had barely seen—Doc and the other—the little rat-faced man-boy—one of them a tattoo artist.

And her vagina!

A steel ring had been set in her. She had been

pierced. After one of them had shaved her pussy completely bare. Both sides of her slit had been pierced and a steel ring attached. She gasped and looked at herself.

"It's permanent—"Frank said—

"The ring can't be taken out—except by cutting it in half. Or ripping it out of you. It's heavy-duty steel. And that's not likely—that it could be cut in half."

Helen stared back and forth—from the black panther tattoo to the ring—to the tattoo, down to the ring.

The panther was crouching, head downward, in an attack mode, its two front paws slightly turned in, as though it was guarding her pussy. It had its mouth open in a growl. It was shiny black, but its eyes and mouth and tongue were blood red. The panther image was quite accurate—

Head down, the crouching panther had its butt up—the base of its spine under her left breast. Its tail began under her left breast, then up, up, into her cleavage, then curled around her left breast, down again, and then cured three-fourths of the way up and ended at her nipple. But she couldn't even see her left nipple. It has been tattooed black and was now the tip of the panther's tail.

She momentarily couldn't find her own navel—it too was tattooed black and was part of the panther, toward the back of its head.

She was too astonished for words—

A massive black panther tattoo on her belly. And chest—the tail was up so far into and over her cleavage—the only way should could hide it would be to wear turtle- neck sweaters anything she wore lower than neck-high would reveal some part of the panther tattoo.

And the ring! Permanently set in her vagina. In her pussy. In her slit.

She was transfixed—she looked at the tattoo— then the ring—then the tattoo—and the padlock earrings.

The panther *was* beautiful—it appeared to be guarding her slit. Snarling. The emblem of the biker club. The snarling panther. On her. Forever.

Then she realized—*she was the emblem of the club*.

A living emblem of the club—a permanent tattoo of the panther on her. She bent forward slightly. She saw the panther crinkle slightly as her skin creased.

The bikers stood around and watched her. She was still too astonished for speech. The tail of the panther, beginning under her left breast, then up, between her breasts, then circling over the top of her left breast, around the breast and even covering her nipple, which was now the tip of the tail.

Astonishing!

And it hadn't hurt. The spray that made her cold and feel so numb—must have been some sort of aerosol kind of Novocain. Or something like it. She had been completely tattooed from her belly to her ribcage and up over her left breast.

And she hadn't felt a thing. Or when the ring was set in place.

"Look—" Frank said. He stood behind her and held her chin up, cupping it so she had to look awkwardly in the mirror.

Something. There was something under her chin. What one of the two men had done. Maybe last. She couldn't see.

Something? Writing? Script? It was hard to tell.

"You can't read it backwards because of the mirror," Frank said.

"Does it look backwards? It's writing. Nice fine script. Shall I read it to you?

PROPERTY OF

"And room for another line under that. A name—someone's name—"

"All anyone will have to do to identify you is tip your chin up."

Words swirled in her mind -

PROPERTY OF

A thing to own—
A possession—
An animal—
Pussy pierced with ring—

PROPERTY OF

"Can't you say something?" Frank asked.

She was suddenly very tired. Exhausted. Traumatized by how she appeared.

"Can't you thank Doc for the nice ring?"

"Oh," he said suddenly, "We forgot—you now have nice new earrings." He pulled her hair back and turned her head a bit sideways to reveal her right ear.

Padlocks. Small padlocks. As earrings. Small rectangular padlocks. Locked into her pierced ears.

"I gave Doc the keys—as souvenirs—

"Can't you thank Doc for the nice ring?" Frank said again.

"—he's very skillful—"

She tried to think of something to say.

"Yes, she said weakly. "thank you very much—"

"Wears 'em out," Doc said, absently, to Frank. "Let her relax for a while. Let her sleep if she wants to. An exhausting rush. You know?—a shock—to discover you'd been tattooed and pierced with a ring. Some of 'em can't comprehend it right away—let her sleep—don't worry—the tattoo is dry. She can sleep on her belly if she wants to. And the ring is antiseptic—surgical steel—no infection problems—"

"Thanks Doc," Frank said.

"Don't forget—part payment for the job—a piece of her when I want I—" He turned to pack up some of his gear.

"I'm sure Helen will be happy to thank you properly any time you want—she'll be delighted to thank you—well, with her mouth now—it's just as soft and wet as a pussy—I'm sure she'd love to thank you for the fine job you did with her ring—"

Frank looked at her.

She had gone to the bed, and was curled up on her side. Naked. Asleep.

Frank laughed, and slapped her butt once.

She didn't move.

The tattoo and the ring in her slit and the tattoo under her chin transformed her practically overnight. She sat in front of the bathroom mirror, on her knees, when Frank was out—she sat for hours at a time, looking at the great black snarling panther on her belly and ribcage and the tail wrapped around her left breast.

She no longer felt the slightest part bitchy. It never again occurred to her. She seldom spoke unless Franks spoke to her. It was as if the bitchy part of her disappeared as the black tattoo was applied to her.

One of the bikers who was a part-time photographer brought a camera and a flash unit one day—Frank had probably suggested it—word had spread through the biker club about her tattoo.

They moved some of the motorcycles away from one wall, sealed the front windows and put a

CLOSED sign on the front door.

They parked a dark redHarley Davidson along one wall. Frank made her pose, in a white garter belt, white stockings and white spike heels, in front of the Harley.

Her legs were spread, and a chrome chain had been padlocked to her ring. It hung to her ankles.

She posed with her legs apart, the ring and padlock and the top of the chain perfectly visible in the photo.

She head the camera click and click again and again.

She straddled the bike, barely standing on the foot pegs, the chain hanging down on the viewer's side.

She was put on her knees in front of the chopper. With her leg apart, the ring that pierced her and the padlock and chain showing perfectly.

On her knees and elbows, her head, down photographed from behind, down the chain hanging down between her legs into a round pile between her knees.

The posing continued.

On her knees, legs apart, holding the chain up, as if to give it to an unseen person.

On her knees, with the chain, almost completely tight held sideways by an arm—a male arm—to the left of the photo.

On her back, with her legs up some, the chain again in a pile near her lock and ring.

On her knees, the chain looped sideways and locked to the engine of the Harley

Nearly naked, locked to a Harley Davidson.

Every biker's wet dream, she thought.

Every photo showed her ring and padlock and the chain clearly.

Many were close-ups.

The photography took all afternoon.

She posed, then sat, then posed again.

Finally, the photographer nodded toward Frank. "Got enough shots?"

Frank nodded. "See you at the club," he said.

Helen remained on her knees.

"Put your hands behind your back."

He stood above her. He put his erection into her mouth.

"We should have had a close-up of this too."

He held her head and slowly, slowly fucked her mouth. She felt drool slide down her chin. He made her gag sometimes. He stopped, sometimes, then rammed his cock into her throat.

He came in her mouth, shooting his hot cum deep into her throat.

She slowly got to her feet—her knees ached.

She leaned again the red Harley.

"You like these bikes better than you like me, don't you Frank?"

It was her last half-hearted attempt at bitchiness.

For that, he chained her to the motorcycle again and let her spend the night alone, in the shop, naked.

She finally fell asleep, her head cradled in her arms, her forearms resting on the gas tank of the chopper. But she only fell half asleep—one part of her stayed awake—to prevent her from falling off the bike.

In the morning she apologized and told him how much she missed sleeping with his cock in her mouth all night. (And she had been truthful—she *had* missed being curled up—his cock in her mouth, her nose nestled in his belly, his pubic hair against her mouth—)

A week or so after she had been pierced, and the ring set in her pussy, and after she had gotten the panther tattoo and the padlocks in her pieced ears, Frank asked her if she's like to work part- ime at the Roamin' Eye, the biker bar, behind the bar. Helen agreed without complaint.

"From six p.m. until closing. The bartender will make the mixed drinks, you handle the bottles or cans of beers. Simple enough?"

"Sure."

The next night Frank took her to the bar at five p.m. He told her to wear the push-up bra she had, and the biker vest and the garter belt and the hose she had bought for the brief time she was supposed to be a topless dancer. She wore the satin miniskirt, that she had also bought. Nothing under her skirt. No panties. She wore only panties when she was locked in Frank's loft by herself; no panties at all when she was out with him—nothing under the cutoffs which showed so much of her butt. Part of the tattoo was visible above her vest, Helen knew, but without taking the vest off, no one could tell what the tattoo was.

When they got to the bar, Helen received her first shock of the night. She had assumed the photos for, were only for Frank's. A private photo session, although she didn't ask him to make them private—she simply assumed he would keep them for himself. But there were three blow-ups of the photos Frank's biker friend had taken—the photos had been blown up to poster size.

The first showed Helen wearing a white garter belt, white stockings and white spike heels, facing the camera, in front of the dark red Harley Davidson. Her tattoo and pussy ring could be clearly seen. A chrome chain, had been locked to the ring and hung between her legs almost to her ankles.

The next shot showed her on a chopper, and it was obvious from the camera angle that she had been chained to the cycle by the ring in her slit.

The third was a blow-up of a close-up shot, from under her navel to above her knees. A medium-sized padlock has been locked into her ring and could be clearly seen hanging from the ring.

Frank took her behind the bar, to meet the regular bartender. Another biker was waiting behind the bar. He had the name Hank on his denim vest.

"Hank works construction sometimes," Frank said. ""He's got something for you." Helen looked at the biker. He held a coil of some steel-like cable. And two padlocks, with the keys inserted in the bottom of each.

"Here," said Frank and guided her to the back of the bar, in the exact center. There were chrome waist-high refrigerted units at each side behind the bar, containing cold beer, she supposed. She looked down—a foot below the top of the bar, on the bartender's side was a steel ring, attached to the bar.

"Come here," he said to Helen and took the cable from Hank."

"This is a light-weight steel alloy. Not heavy, but unbreakable."

Both ends of the coil of cable had metal loops. Frank locked one end of the cable to the ring in the bar. The he lifted her skirt and slipped the second padlock through her ring and locked her to the cable.

She was flushed with wave after wave of humiliation.

She said nothing, but tried as modestly as she could to smooth her skirt down n front.

"Lookin' good," Hank said to Frank.

"I owe you one for the cable," Frank said to him.

"I'll take it out from your chick sometime when she isn't busy—"

"How about it Helen?" Frank said, "do you want to thank him for the cable?"

Helen looked at hem as proudly as she could.

"It's not possible to get into my pussy with the ring in place, but I'll try to thank him as well as I can, Frank."

"Nicely trained now," Frank said offhandedly to the other biker. "All she needed was the ring and the tattoo."

Frank warned her *not* to lift up her skirt and show anybody the ring and how the cable was locked to her, but everyone would soon know—and all of them couldn't miss the poster-sized pictures of her.

The bar slowly filled up. Helen tested the cable. She as at first afraid that it would pull the ring out of her slit, but the cable was lightweight and the ring didn't seen to be stressed much by the weight of the cable.

The bar was about 18 feet long; the cable was about seven feet, so Helen could only work in the middle of the bar. She got used to the tug when she reached the end of the cable; when it got taut, she moved back toward the middle of the bar. She could move left or right only the length of the cable. When she was standing in the middle of the bar, the cable hung loose from under her skirt and the slack dropped to the floor.

She has to watch to step over it, so she didn't trip on the slack on the floor.

All in all, it wasn't bad, but she felt a constant warmth, a glow, through her, especially up from inside her pussy and she thought constantly about the ring in her slit and how the cable hung from underneath her skirt and how she was now tethered to the bar and could only move a few feet to the right or left, before she was stopped by the cable.

The warmth never left her—*when the erotic meets humiliation,* she thought—*when humiliation meets the erotic.* She was at that point now and there was no telling how long this would last for her.

At about 9 p.m., Frank suddenly stood upon the bar. Some of the bikers had apparently discovered Helen's cable by accident. Frank made it official. "I have something to tell you—You met my chick here earlier. She's going to work the bar most nights. But you guys have to order from the center of the bar—"

He turned to Helen. "Climb up on the bar onto your knees and tell 'em why."

She had an unopened can of beer in one hand. She had to wait for the bartender to get her a chair. She took a deep breath and held the bartender's elbow. She climbed awkwardly onto the bar, onto her knees. Her knees were instantly hurt by the hard edge of the bar.

She had to make sure the chain hung down between her legs. She had to make sure the chain would reach that far—she looked down to one side—there was some slack left.

"I—Frank—" she looked out into a sea of bikers—probably three or four dozen—she thought.

"Frank wanted me to wear a *ummm ahhh*— under my skirt (she tried to skip over the word *ring*) and I'm ahhh—locked to the back of the bar by this cable and it's about seven feet long," She was better when she was past the ring part.

"I've got about six feet of slack in this cable—it goes up my skirt and if you want me to get you a beer or something, you'll have to ask at the middle of the bar, Or else I can't reach you—"

She tentatively touched the cable at the hem of her skirt.

"What's she's trying to say is that she's got a ring in her pussy and that she'd padlocked to that cable," Frank said.

Helen felt another wash of warmth and humiliation flow through her.

He didn't have to tell them so graphically, she thought.

"You who haven't seen the posters near the pool tables—that's Helen about two weeks ago just after she got tattooed.

"Tell 'em all what the tattoo is—"

"It's the club's black panther," she said, "and he's snarling and guarding my ring—although you can't see it—his tail ends here—" She cupped her hand over her left breast—

Frank added—"the end of the panther's tail is her tit. Her nipple, One of these days she'll show it to you. But you can check out in the posters—" There was a murmur of approval.

"Remember if you need anything, she can't get any farther from the middle of the bar than about six feet. But you can get a good look at how's she's padlocked—if you stand at the side of the bar." There were a few shouts of *Padlock. Padlock.* Before she could realize it, that became her nickname. No one after that called her by her name. She had to answer to *Padlock* (Later Frank had the word *Padlock* embroidered on the top left of her biker vest.)

"I almost forgot," Frank said with amusement, "what's your smaller tattoo say?" he forced her head up by lifting her chin. "Check it out guys—when you're close enough—"

"It says 'Property of—,'"she said softly.

"Louder babe, they can't hear you—"

"Property of—" she said, "tattooed under my chin.

"And some word or two to be added later—"

Then he almost *did* forgot—then turned her head and slowly pulled her hair away from her left ear. She had almost forgotten too—the small rectangular padlocks, in her pierced ears.

"They can't be taken off—the keys have been lost—" Frank said. "And it's impossible to get any sort of cutting tool that close to her ears—her ears would have to be surgically cut to get the locks out—"

After that, most of the bikers came to the middle of the bar when they needed beer. Helen left the other bartender mix the mixed drinks—she handled the beer and made change for the pinball games.

Almost all of the bikers wanted to read the tattoo on her chin; most of them called her *Padlock* then, and a few of them stood at the end of the bar, where they could watch her behind the bar, watch the cable lift and fall as she walked from the center of the bar, putting more stress in the cable and lifting it off of the floor.

She noticed that the biker women didn't come close—they stayed as far away as possible—apparently, Helen thought, that if they showed any interest at all, the men would do the same to them. Pierced, with a ring inserted, on a chain. Tattooed—or—?

When she returned to the center of the bar, the slack in the cable caused it to drop onto the floor. She had to be careful then not to trip on it; she had to step over it carefully or pull it so it hung in front of her, or step over it and make sure it hung slightly behind her.

Almost like having a tail, she thought.

She felt the cable pull at the ring so deeply piercing her, but she was no longer worried. The cable was so light that it wouldn't tear out of her, unless she somehow tried quickly to go farther than the length of the cable permitted. And even then, it would be difficult for the ring to be pulled out of her.

She worked the bar every night, from six until it closed. Some of the bikers got there early, when they discovered her hours, and they asked her to describe to them how it felt to get tattooed—so completely all over her chest and belly and how she felt when she knew what the tattoo said under her chin. And were the padlocks in her ears too heavy? *I got used to them*, she said, *I don't notice them anymore.*

They seemed to want to know *everything* about the ring in her slit.

Frank had promised her that she wouldn't have to hold up her skirt to show the ring and how the cable was locked into the ring with a padlock, but eventually he forgot that promise.

The bikers wanted to know everything. If it ever hurt—how she could pee with the ring so tightly into her.

"How does your old man fuck you now?" one of the bikers asked bluntly. It was a common question—in a variety of words—usually obscene.

"Just like before," she said, "he gets it when he wants it," but obviously that wasn't true, except not exactly the way the biker believed.

He believed it was possible—somehow—for her to get fucked with the ring in place, but she knew it wasn't possible. No way.

What she didn't tell him was that just after the ring was inserted—the next day, as she remembered, she had to pee. The bath in the loft was only a half-bath—a commode and a small sink. A metal factory-type shower in downstairs, behind the motorcycle parts area of Frank's shop.

She went to the commode—and discovered that the ring was set deeply into her that she couldn't pee. Not at all—siting normally. She began to panic—it's wasn't even possible to even pee normally.

She rushed to Frank, when he returned.

"Frank, Frank—I—can't—just can't—"

"Can't what?"

"I can't pee anymore. I have to go but the ring keeps me so tight—"

Frank knew. Doc had told him while she was sedated.

She even let him watch her try—on the commode—that most intimate of women's functions. She would normally be mortified if a man watched her pee, but she couldn't help it—now.

"I can't—now—like this—"

He snapped a dog leash on the ring and told her to follow.

As if she had a choice—following him or not—she knew she wouldn't dare unsnap the leash and having to pee was crucial now anyway—

He led her downstairs to the dingy shower.

"Squat—you can probably pee in that position—it puts more pressure on your insides—"

She *was* able to pee like that.

And after that, when she had to pee, she'd have to ask him. To take her down to the shower, where she could spread her feet and pee into the shower drain.

Sometimes he'd take her outside and let her

squat behind the shop, peeing outside. Hoping no one would possibly see her.

And then—she got her period. And realized that she couldn't possibly insert a tampon. She could barely insert her little finger part-way at the bottom of her slit. She wouldn't be able to use a tampon—at all.

"Frank—" she said, pleading—"you'll have to get me some of those—adult diapers—you know—for people who—*ahhh*—leak a little."

Sure he said, but he usually forgot. *Always conveniently forget*, she thought—and then she'd have to hold a towel between her legs during her period.

The first night, after she worked tethered to the bar by the cable, and the padlock, into her ring, she was so hot, so excited, so wet, that when she got to Frank's loft, she told him how hot and wet she was. He laughed at her. Then she offered to suck and fuck him. Again he laughed. He told her that he'd possess her when *he* wanted to, not when she was ready.

She slid a little finger into the bottom of her slit and told him how wet she was—then she begged him—she pleaded with him to somehow screw her. To rape her. She used all the words she knew, for all the acts she could think of. She wanted him so badly,

She thought she might climax standing right in front of him. She took off her mini-skirt and her vest and push-up bra and showed him her nipples were hard.

He finally took her to the side of the loft where he had the pulleys hanging from the ceiling. He bound her arms behind her back, as he had done before, with ropes from her wrists to her elbows. He made her kneel, put a heavy black leather dog collar on her with a heavy ring set at the back of her neck.

He used a pulley and a rope to hold her up straight, then he gagged her with a pair of her own panties and put duct tape over her mouth, roped her legs above the knees and at the ankles, and left her kneeling, naked and bound, totally un-fucked, un-screwed in anyway, for the night.

She dozed off now and then. Finally when she thought her arms and knees couldn't stand it anymore, Frank came back to her, untied the rope that held her head upright, took off the duct tape and pulled her panties out of her mouth. She expected him to take her mouth. She would welcome even that. But he didn't

"You get it when I want it—" he said, 'not when you're hot. "Understand—?"

"Yes, yes, sir," she said, hoping, praying that he would take her then. But he left her bound and naked, kneeling until she had to dress and go to work again.

It made her so excited talking with the bikers in the bar. When she got to the bar that second night, she knew that she would have to stand still to be tethered to the cable again. Frank usually locked the padlock to the ring in her slit.

He made her stand behind the bar. There were five or six bikers, drinking beer at the bar. They knew what was coming—what she had to do. As discreetly as she could, she turned her back to the bikers, while she was waiting for Frank to straighten out the cable and get the padlock ready.

"Hey," one biker said, "can't see—" Frank was on one knee, working with the cable. He looked up at her. "Turn around—"

He pushed her so she had to stand facing the bikers.

"Get your skirt up—" she had to stand waiting for him with her skirt up to her waist, giving all the bikers a perfect view of her slit and the ring.

Finally Frank padlocked her ring to the cable. She thought she would climax right there, she was so wet, after all the bikers watched her get padlocked to the cable and the bar for the night.

She thought she'd climax again, right there, she was so wet, after all the bikers at the bar watched her get padlocked for the night. She felt herself flush with wave after wave of warmth. If she kept this up much longer she knew she'd climax right on the spot.

After the bikers got tired of watching her and

dispersed momentarily, she bent down, under the counter to check supplies. But she really checked herself. She reached under her skirt with one hand. The inside of her thighs were wet. She knew it—she was wet almost to her knees.

Just thinking about how she was padlocked to the cable, with nothing on under her skirt.

Talking with the bikers and even taunting hem now and then, made her wetter. Terribly wet. She thought she might come right behind the bar.

Maybe she always wanted to be like this.

Pierced. Ringed. Tattooed, padlocked to a small area where she had to work behind the bar—it just made her wetter and wetter to think about it.

Frank let her wear the biker's vest—only now he had the name *Padlock* embroidered on the vest above her left breast.

Or he let her wear a bikini top to work. One night he gave her a pair of topless dancer's pasties and made her work all night without nothing on above her waist except the pasties, so the bikers could see almost all of her tattoo, except the part that disappeared below her waist, under her skirt.

Sometimes she wore a turtle-neck sweater, which completely covered her arms and torso and neck, but even then, all the bikers had to do to remind themselves what she looked like was to walk across the bar to the giant posters Frank had put up near the pool tables.

She couldn't wait to get home where he hopped Frank would—somehow—take her wet pussy or her mouth, where she hopes he'd rape her if he wanted: then she couldn't wait to get back to the bar where she knew she'd be padlocked again. Naked under her skirts, the padlock firmly snapped into the ring in her slit, her naked shaved pussy, which was guarded permanently by the snarling panther, the tattoo which she knew was the symbol of the biker club.

One night when she got to work, there was a sign over the bar and another near the pool tables.

AUCTION TONIGHT

She asked Frank what it meant, as he was locking her behind the bar.

"We sometimes have these auctions. After hours. We close the place for the night and lock the doors. You'll see later."

She was too busy all night to wonder much more about it. She talked with the bikers at the bar and taunted one or two of them; she had to be careful to keep from tripping over the cable.

When the bar closed at the end of the night, she had forgotten about the signs. Frank locked the front door, then climbed onto the middle of the bar.

"I think it's time we had an auction—" he said.

There were about 36 or so bikers in the bar, some with their women, some

"We start at $100 and work down—and the little item to be auctioned off—for the rest of the night—is Padlock."

She stood dumbfounded. Auctioned off. For someone's use, for the rest of the night. She couldn't quite believe it. One of the guys leaned over the bar.

"You've never seen one of our auctions, babe. If the guys see what they like, then the bidding goes down fast. The idea is to buy the pussy for the night as cheap as possible. That shows her that she ain't worth as much as she thinks. Usually the girls are sold for $5 a night, and they are expected to work their tails off. Trick after trick, see?"

She knew what he meant. *A trick*, she knew was slang. For screwing. What hookers did. *Turning a trick*. And she's be expected to turn a trick all night. For one of the bikers, who bought her at an auction. A reverse auction.

"Get up here," Frank said and grabbed her and helped her getup on the bar,

"Who starts the bidding for a night with this pussy—Miss College-Educated—Miss Padlock?"

The bidding went quickly from $100 to $75 to $50 to $45 to $40 and down—then she heard a voice.

"She may not work out very well for your guys with that ring in place—you usually don't give us a chance to bid - but why not? Maybe all she's good for is eating pussy."

It was Honey. The girl who was whipped as she and Helen hung together belly to belly in the loft.

Honey pushed her way to the edge of the bar.

"How about it, guys?"

There was a murmur throughout the bar. Apparently the women didn't usually participate in this kind of auction.

"OK guys—can Honey bid tonight?" One of them yelled, "Let her bid."

It seemed to the bikers to be their own idea of a good joke.

"Whatdya bid, Honey?"

"Being that she's ringed and probably tired from working all night—69 cents."

The bikers laughed at the double meaning.

"You got her, Honey, for all the rest of the night—in my loft—for 69 cents.".

Honey got change from the other bartender and solemnly gave Frank 69 cents.

He remained standing on the bar and Honey had to reach up to give him he change—all the bikers could see that she paid Frank for Padlock—for the night. For 69 cents.

When the bar closed, Helen rode home on the back of Frank's chopper, as usual. Honey's man brought her to the loft.

"Wanta watch?" he asked Frank.

"Not fair," Honey said, "the girls don't get to

watch when you guys win some pussy for the night—"
Frank laughed. "Let's go—let Honey have her for the
rest of the night—" The two bikers left. The women
could hear them lock the stair door on the outside.

"Thanks" Helen said, "For saving me—I don't
know what one of those guys would have made me
do—"

"I was auctioned off one night last year," Honey
volunteered.

"To two guys, For $5 for both. They just worked
me over all night—all my openings—my pussy and
ass and mouth. I was sore and exhausted for a week.
One then the other then the first again. Finally both
at once. I was on a big wet spot on a mattress and
couldn't move. I was a mess—"

Helen thought it awful. She put on a clean pair
of panties but kept the biker t-shirt on, that she had
worn that night in the bar. Honey had pulled off her
clothes and had gotten into the bed. "I always sleep in
the buff—how about you?"

"I like to have something on, but Frank always
makes me sleep naked, but I never really much sleep
like that—"

Helen curled up next to Honey.

"Remember—when we were tied together—you
said wouldn't it nice if we could just cuddle up all
warm and nice and just sleep?"

"I remember," Honey said, "but not tonight. I'm
hot."

She looked at Helen and cupped Helen's chin with one hand.

"I did buy you—slide down and lie between my legs—Go on—now." Honey lay on her back with her legs spread.

"But Honey—"

"Now, babe—"

Helen slid down and curled up under the covers. It was nice and warm and Honey smelled good. She must have some perfume on her belly. Helen kissed the insides of Honey's legs. Her thighs.

Just one more minute and I'll try to lick her— Helen thought. *I'm so tired. I'll have to try and please her in a minute—and—and—*

She fell asleep.

It seemed like years later—she was so tired she could barely move. She did move finally, slowly climbing out of the covers. Empty. The bed was empty. She looked around. Honey was sitting at the small breakfast bar in the kitchen area of the loft, with a cup of instant coffee.

"Honey—I—"

Honey looked at her.

"Some deal you are. You fell asleep two seconds after you crawled into that bed—"

Helen was ashamed. She did want to—

"I'll—I'm sorry—I—well, now, right now, if you want—I'll—"

She didn't know how to tell Honey that she

would, would do what she should have done. Last night, but she had been so tired.

"The guys will be back any time now, babe—" Honey said, cross now with Helen. "You lost your chance. I didn't get even 69 cents worth of you—"

"Honey," Helen said, "don't be cross with me— I'm sorry I fell asleep—"

But Honey was pissed.

"The first time I've been away from my man in months—I wanted to make it with you—and you had to fall asleep—"

"But," Helen said, "why didn't you try to wake me?"

"I tried, but you were out. *O-U-T.* I couldn't budge you."

"Maybe next time—"Helen said.

"There won't be a next time. I had my chance with you—it'll be someone else's turn next. One of the guys—"

The bikers returned. Honey left with her man, still pissed at Helen for falling asleep and spoiling the evening.

That night, at the bar, after she was tethered to the cable, the bikers gathered around her, 12 or 15, maybe, all wanting to know what happened. She didn't want to say. Honey and her man showed up then, far earlier than they had ever arrived before.

Honey walked to the bar. It looked to Helen as if Honey was still pissed.

"How was it, Honey?" one of the bikers asked. "Was your pussy worth it?"

"She wasn't worth anything—" Honey said, "she feel asleep and I couldn't wake her up. She wasn't worth 69 cents."

Frank was standing behind the bar, beside Helen.

"Is that right Padlock?" he asked—"didn't you give her anything she paid for? All 69 cents worth?"

Helen looked pleadingly at Frank—" but I *was* so tired—I tried—but I did fall asleep—I didn't want to Frank—I did want to do her—I would have—"

Frank dug into his pocket and pulled out some change. And put it on the bar.

"Here's your money back Honey. She'll have to learn about not behaving. You can help. I'll let you know. At the loft. Sometime soon."

Honey scooped the change from the bar. "Thanks Frank." It looked to Helen that Honey would never forgive her for falling asleep.

Frank took her out one afternoon to a lingerie shop and bought her a knee-length transparent light blue nightgown. It was lovely. He bought her and a matching blue camisole which had a half-cup bra. And he bought her a separate matching garter belt and light stockings. And matching four inch spike high heels. She put the camisole on the first time she got back to the loft. She loved the feel—(Bikers would have no idea how to ask for that for their women.)

She loved the feel—the secure safe, warm feeling the bra cups gave to her breasts. She put on her stockings and hooked them to her garter belt. And put on the nightie.

"Nice," Frank said, "very nice. Oh, incidentally—remember—your punishment for falling asleep with Honey? Friday night. You and me and Honey and a man from San Francisco. You can wear this outfit—" he paused.

"We'll be making a film—a videotape—Here. In the loft. A crew also from San Francisco. They do these things regularly. You'll be the star."

He pulled the nightie open. She wore nothing from her waist down. Her pussy and ring could easily be seen.

"You'll enjoy it," he said, "Maybe."

Helen had Friday off—she wouldn't be working at the bar because of the video-taping. Late in the afternoon, she took a shower (Frank led her to the shower on her dog leash). She washed her hair and dried it with a hair dryer, which Frank had scrounged up somewhere. She didn't know quite what else to do—so she put on the camisole and stockings, carefully smoothing them and hooking them into the garter belt She put on the matching nightgown and spike heels and waited.

Frank had gone somewhere and locked the loft when he left.

He finally came back with a package from a convenience store. A six-pack of cold beer.

"Here," he said, popping one, "have one." She sipped at the cold beer.

"Frank, what's going to happen tonight?"

He looked at her. "We're making a film—on videotape."

"I know—what's the story?"

"It's better if you don't know. More exciting." He didn't volunteer any more. So she waited and waited, sitting on the bed in her camisole, nightgown, garter belt and spike heels.

Honey and her man finally arrived. "Hi!" Honey said, brightly. Honey's man had some beer of his own.

"I have to change—" Honey said, and walked to the small half-bath. She was carrying a duffle bag over one shoulder.

The film crew arrived, three men carrying lights, tripods and cameras and other equipment.

They conferred with Frank, then set up floodlights—the lights illuminated the side of the loft with the pulleys which hung from the ceiling.

Another man entered, a tall non-biker looking man, with a vague foreign appearance, wearing leather pants, and a leather jacket. He nodded to Frank. Honey re-appeared from the bathroom.

She wore thigh-high boots, a black mini-skirt, black elbow-length gloves, a black half-cup bra and a black mask. The man who came last walked to the bathroom.

A minute or so later he reappeared. Wearing nothing more than boots, leather pants which and a mask like Honey's. Bare-chested. He and Frank called Honey over to them. They spoke quietly to each other as if they were planning something. Honey's man stood at one side of the loft.

Helen watched the camera crew set up their tripods, cameras and gear. It looked like they would have one camera on a tripod and a second to held on one crew man's shoulder.

She was right—the tripod was set up facing the pulley area and the lights were set in a semi-circle, on the left and right of the tripod, also facing the pulley area.

Helen stood off to the left, behind the stage lights. Honey came over and snapped a dog leash into Helen's ring.

"I'll walk you into the scene—in front of the cameras—in front of the pulleys. You do what I tell you to do and say 'yes ma'am or 'no ma'am'. And say it like you mean it.

"But Honey—"

Honey looked at her and gave her a sharp smack on her behind. Hard.

"*Beginning now*. Let's try this again. And don't you think of using my name when this begins. Now— she said—"I'll walk you into exactly the right spot— and stand with your legs apart."

"Yes ma'am," Helen said. She suddenly realized that Honey had done this before. And knew exactly what to do and what to say.

She heard the camera crew test their sound system with the usual "test one, testing, test two, test three—"

One of the cameramen nodded toward Frank.

"OK—"

Frank nodded to Honey.

Bright stage lights came on—two on the left of the camera and two on the right.

"I'll lead you out there on your leash—

"When we're out there, you stand still—you do what I say. Immediately. I'll take your robe off and your top off (Honey probably didn't know the word *camisole*, Helen thought)—after that—no sweat, OK?"

"Yes ma'am," Helen said, not wanting to get another smack on her butt from Honey.

Honey smiled at her, and looked at Frank. "Now?"

"Now."

Honey led Helen into the lights, on her dog leash, in front of where the video camera on the tripod would be and about three feet in front of the pulleys near the wall. And turned Helen toward the camera.

The lights were so bright Helen could see nothing past the lights—she didn't know where Frank or

Honey's man might be—all she saw were the blinding stage lights in her face.

Honey stood slightly beside her and slowly spread Helen's nightgown open, then slowly took it off. Then she slowly took off Helen's camisole.

"Turn around," Honey said.

"Yes ma'am."

Helen faced the wall. She felt Honey slowly caress her behind, one side then the other, slowly, slowly.

"Turn back around."

"Yes ma'am—" Helen again faced the blinding stage lights.

She could not see, but the man in the black mask and black leather pants entered the scene. He held something in his hand.

He walked enough into the scene that Helen could see him sideways—she didn't have to try and see behind the blinding stage lights.

Then Helen saw what he had. She knew what they were, the padded leather handcuffs that had been put on her earlier.

The man reached up, behind Helen and pulled the cable down, snapped on one cuff, then the other. He stepped out of the picture momentarily. Helen felt her wrists being pulled up, up, up.

Her arms were pulled above her head. Not severely tightly, but enough so she couldn't move much. She looked toward the cameras, trying to see them behind the blinding stage lights.

She felt Honey's hands on her. She looked down. Honey was spreading her legs slightly, so one camera could—*probably, she thought*—get a close-up shot of the ring in her pussy.

Honey fingered it, tugging it slightly. Helen couldn't see because of the lights, but a camera was then panning up to get a close-up shot of her panther tattoo. Honey softly ran a fingertip up from the panther's body, to the base of its tail, then between Helen's breasts, following the tail, up her breast around her left breast, to her nipple, which had become the tip of the tail.

The masked, bare-chested man returned and snapped a dog leash to Helen's labia ring. Then he stepped back, tightening the tension on the leash. Helen felt the leash pull at her ring. He gave the leash to Honey, then stepped out of the picture again.

Helen felt the cables pull. She was pulled up until only her toes were on the floor. Helen could feel Honey pulling on the leash. She was afraid the ring would be ripped out of her pussy. She took a couple of small tentative steps forward, trying to loosen the tension on the ring in her slit.

Honey tugged again.

Helen yipped with pain. Honey let the leash slacken, then tugged again, this time harder. Helen shook her head, trying to fight the pain in her slit. Again Honey tugged at the leash, harder than before.

Helen felt herself being pulled forward. She cried out in pain.

The pain was stronger—Honey again pulled harder on the leash.

She felt the man again, behind her, man cupping each breast. She was powerless to protect her breasts or her ring. The man behind her slapped each breast. Then he jiggled each breast—then slapped them, again. Harder.

She cried out in pain again. Honey tugged the leash again, then held tension on the leash. Honey tugged quickly, again and again. Helen cried again, louder.

The man reached down and pinched Helen's butt. She yipped and jumped toward Honey. Momentarily the leash slackened, so Honey tugged again, pulling on the ring. Helen was sure, sure, that she would be mutilated. The ring would be torn from her—ripping her! She was sure—she began a low moan.

Suddenly Honey walked toward her and unsnapped the leash from her ring, and dropped the leash onto the floor.

Honey held some something—*or somethings*—toward the camera. Helen trued to see what it might be, but the camera lights were in her eyes. Honey gave one of the things—*what were they?*—to the bare-chested man, who ha stepped back into camera range.

Then he spun her around, so she was sideways to the camera. He showed he what he had. A flat leather paddle—it was about four inches wide and about 12 inches long. Toward the base it tapered to a handle.

He stepped behind Helen and swung.

She felt the paddle bite into her behind. She jumped with sudden pain. Again the paddle caught her butt. She shook on the cable holding her nearly off the ground. She did a small dance, trying to keep her toes on the floor.

Again the paddle caught her with a loud crack.

The man was right on target, in the middle of her behind. The spanking caught her butt, time after time, exactly on the center of her behind. Time after time.

Helen began to cry, each time the paddle hit her behind.

She began to wonder how much of this she could stand. She felt her behind burning, hot, hot, from the constant paddling.

The man began a rhythm of strokes—one after another—time after time after time.

If anything the blows were harder than before. Helen felt her behind quivering with pain.

She shook her head, cried, then began whimpering. He took a moment then to knead her behind.

Then again—the hardest blow yet. Helen cried out—then again and again. Blow after blow.

Then the man turned her so she faced away from the cameras. Helen did not realize, then, that the cameras were getting perfect close-ups of her reddened behind.

Turned toward the wall, Helen looked to the left trying to see Honey.

Honey! Honey held one of the paddles. Then Honey and the man in the mask both began paddling her, one after the other. As one would smack her, then the other would be swinging toward her.

The man disappeared. And Honey stopped her own swings. Momentarily Helen was alone, gasping and trying to recover.

Was this the end? Was this finally over?

The bare-chested man with the mask stepped back into the picture. Helen saw what he was carrying something else. She didn't know what it was—a long handle of some kind. It looked like a golf club without the club head. A golf club with the club head cut off and the end rounded smooth, with a leather handle.

The man tapped it in his hand. Helen continued to face the cameras. The man stepped back. Helen momentarily heard a *swish* as he swung the rod.

Then she screamed. The rod seemed to cut her behind in two. The pain was 10 times—20 times—stronger than the paddles the man and Honey had been using on her.

Unbearable pain.

She shook from head to toe, swinging on the cable. She swung so much from the force of the blow that her toes left the floor.

Honey held Helen steady. Again Helen's toes touched the floor. Waves of pain shot through her.

And again! He whipped her again with the rod. She threw her head back and cried with the pain and shook uncontrollably. She felt tears in the corners of her eyes. Honey stepped forward, pulled Helen's head down and kissed her. Helen felt Honey's tongue in her mouth.

Then Honey stepped away.

Again the rod kissed her behind. And the rod kissed her. Helen screamed loudly. The rod cut her again and again. And again. She lost count of the times she was whipped.—she just barely had time to hear the rod whistle through the air before it made her scream and scream.

The man stopped once while Honey put a ball gag in Helen's mouth and strapped it into her, with a leather strap. Then the rod again.

She jumped and screamed behind her gag but only a low moan could be heard. The man who had been whipping her turned her around so her behind was toward the cameras. He pried her behind apart slowly. Helen tried to clench of the muscles of her behind, but she couldn't prevent the man from showing how she had been whipped.

Honey was beside her.

"How ya doin'?"

She took the gag out of Helen's mouth.

"Please—please—I have to pee so bad—" Helen

thought she couldn't stand another wave of pain from the crop, without having to pee hanging from the cable. Honey said something to the man, who still had his hands on Helen's behind.

Helen was turned around again. Honey stepped off camera and got an enamelware bowl. The man who had been whipping her lowered the cable—so Helen was able to squat—still with her arms over her head. It wasn't very comfortable, but she could squat.

Helen squatted momentarily, then her pee gushed out of her in a long steady stream. One of the camera men came closer for a shot of her peeing. Then he moved up so he could get a shot of her face, then back down to where she was still peeing. She felt a bit relieved—but ached so—her behind was on fire.

She had long ago lost count of the number of times she had been paddled, then whipped with the rod.

Her pee stopped. The man pulled the cable and lifted her up again so she was on her toes again. He whopped her another five times with the rod, until she was screaming, and thrashing her legs and shaking her head.

Suddenly her head slumped, her chin down.

She was lowered until she was on her knees. The cable was removed from her wrist cuffs, then the cuffs were taken off. Honey had to hold her so she didn't collapse to one side or the other. The man who had been whipping her stood behind her. Helen was groggy with pain.

Honey held her head up.

"Open your legs—" Helen was on her knees. The man whipped her once more, diagonally across her behind.

Helen screamed again, then separated her knees, and leaned forward on her hands and knees.

"Up," said Honey and Helen got off her hands and and sat on her heels, with her knees spread slightly. Honey got the dog leash again. She snapped the link onto the ring in Helen's labia.

"Walk. On your hands and knees—"

Helen learned forward, onto her hands and knees. Honey fed the dog leash between Helen's legs and slowly walked beside Helen as she crawled across the floor, the dog leash up between her legs in the cleft of her behind, then toward Honey's hand.

Helen slowly crawled out of camera range. The film was over. Honey made her crawl to the other side of the loft, to the bed. Helen painfully edged herself onto the bed and collapsed onto her belly. Honey dropped the dog leash onto Helen's behind without unsnapping it.

It took Helen several days just to recover from the exhaustion of the paddling and the whipping— The welts on her behind took much longer to heal— some of them never did disappear.

Frank took her to the Roamin' Eye once and made her put on a bikini bottom when she got there.

She didn't work behind the bar, but Frank did parade her through the bar so all the bikers could see that she had been whipped.

The bikini bottom showed practically everything. she wore her biker vest and high boots. One of the bikers slapped her ass. She jumped and tried to cover her behind with her hands. She was still very sore and the welts very painful.

All the bikers had apparently heard about the video shooting session.

"When you gonna' let us see it, Frank?" one asked.

"Soon," Frank said, "in a few weeks. She'll be a real star, won't you Padlock?'

She looked at Frank and the biker who slapped her ass.

"I hope you'll like it—"

"You'll never forget it, will you?" The biker taunted her.

"No" Helen said, simply and truthfully.

She would never forget how she had been tripped, hung from the ceiling. paddled and then whipped with that terrible rod the man had. She thought during the the video-taping or filming or whatever it was, taping she was going to be sick to her stomach, he hit he so hard. And she peed. She hurt so bad. She remembered every second of it.

A few weeks later, Frank took her to the Nob Hill area of San Francisco, to an exclusive condo building. She didn't know where they were going to why—she wore the only pair of designer jeans that hadn't been cut into the briefest of cut-offs and a black t-shirt. On the top, in gold was the Harley emblem and under it were two lines

Screw Everything
Let's Ride

Frank had borrowed a four-year old car for the occasion, owned by the wife of a biker buddy. She then felt very much out of place there, even though she once had a respectable job and dressed well and lived well in San Francisco, They had to wait for the security staff to buzz the underground parking garage gate open—to keep out all invited guests.

Frank and Helen took an elevator from the underground parking garage to a condo on the tenth floor and were ushered in by a man with a goatee wearing black slacks and a black shirt. Helen had never seen such an expensive place—furniture in grey with chrome trim and a spectacular view of the Bay.

They were joined by a woman in a similar outfit, black knee-length skirt, black sweater, black spike heels. She looked to be about 45 or so—with black hair streaked with grey. She wore no jewelry except two gold hoop earrings. She looked no only older, but more mature, wiser.

The man with the goatee got Frank a drink from a bar inset in one wall.

"You're the one they call Padlock, aren't you?' the woman asked, taking Helen by the arm.

"Yes.

"Your real name is Helen?"

Helen nodded.

"I'll call you Padlock because everyone else does—"

The woman paused momentarily.

"We have known Frank for some time—he was here a few days ago and he brought over the outfit, which you wore in the film. Would you model it for us?"

Helen looked at Frank. She knew this innocent question was a command.

"It's in the bathroom—I'll show you."

Helen walked to a small half-bathroom. On the toilet lid was her camisole, a pair of stockings, her garter belt and the blue nightgown.

"Join us when you're dressed. Leave your clothes here, please." She closed the door as Helen began taking her clothes off.

Helen put her camisole on, the garter belt, the stockings and finally her nightgown. She joined the two men and the woman in the living room.

"Please—" the woman said, "one more thing."

The woman held out a pair of padded handcuffs, joined by four inches of chain.

"Your wrists, Padlock, behind your back, please."

Helen put her wrists together and silently stood as the woman walked behind her and strapped her wrists into the handcuffs. Then the woman walked in front of her again and parted the nightgown.

"Your ring is very nice—" she said, then left Helen momentarily, walked to an end table and returned with a dog leash.

She snapped it into the ring in Helen's labia.

"I'm sure you'll feel better now—much more comfortable."

The two men got up. Helen was escorted to a second large living room. Against one wall was a large-screen flat TV with a video recorder under it.

"We have your film ready, Padlock. We thought you'd like to see it—"

The men took seats, Helen followed the woman to a sofa near the TV.

"On your knees, please Padlock, in front of me."

The woman sat on the sofa Helen awkwardly knelt in front of the woman, on the floor.

One of the men pushed a remote.

The screen flashed. The title appeared—

TATTOOED & TAMED

Helen sat fascinated, watching the film. She saw herself being undressed, her wrists chained above her head. She saw a close-up of the ring in her labia, Honey's hands fingering it, then the camera pulled up and held for a long time, a close-up of her panther tattoo, up, up until the camera showed the tail of her panther tattoo, ending at her nipple.

Then—Helen remembered it—Honey had pulled and pulled on her ring. She had attached the dog leash to Helen's labia ring and Honey had pulled on it so much.

Helen remembered how she thought the ring would be pulled out of her. It pulled so hard on her flesh! Then the man with the mask was taking her camisole off, then slapping each breast. There was no soundtrack—no real music—nothing except the sounds of her being paddled.

Her cries, her moans, her whimpering from the paddling. And the occasional sounds of the chains when she was twisting and thrashing from the paddling.

Helen felt herself get wet—wet from watching herself and wet from being nearly naked in front of Frank and these two strangers.

The woman on the sofa leaned down.

"You're exciting to watch. Do you remember it all?

Helen nodded. "Yes," she said quietly.

The woman on the sofa reached down and slid one hand under Helen's nightgown. Helen felt one little finger slide up and down over her slit, then into the bottom of her slit, and out again. She was wet!

Watching herself on the screen. The woman held her hand in front of Helen's face.

"You're wet and juicy—do you know that?"

Helen nodded. The men were watching the film. Helen was being paddled now, by Honey and the man in the mask, one then the other.

Helen saw her own flesh shake and quiver. Then part of it was in slow motion, showing her butt shake as she was paddled, one blow after another. Coming now in slow motion.

Then the speed picked up again. Helen saw herself kissing Honey's pussy. Then again—Then the man with the mask re-appeared in the film. He had the chrome rod—the golf-club like rod which had made such welts and scars on her behind.

"That's Werner. He's very good, isn't he?"

The woman said softly to Helen. Helen didn't know what to say in reply. She was watching herself on the screen.

"He's very good. He's a very stringent master.

"He knows exactly how much—where to apply the rod and when to stop—" the woman said, as if the two were having a casual conversation about their tastes in fashion.

"I've seen this before Padlock—you're very good. I counted. But I'll let you count how many times if you like—we can play it again and you an count the strokes—how many do you think?"

"No—please, ma'am. I'd rather not know."

She watched herself being whipped by the chrome rod. One after another, red welts began to appear on her behind.

Instant red welts. One or two dripped a drop of blood. Time after time. The rod made her behind shake and quiver so. The camera panned back as she thrashed on her chains, her toes barely on the floor.

The woman's fingers continued to probe in her slit. She felt herself get wetter and wetter.

She looked at Frank once—he was watching her, not the film. She was as wet as she had ever been.

She remembered when Honey put the gag in her mouth. And remembered how she couldn't scream— only moan behind the gag.

Helen watched herself on the screen—she remembered how she had to pee. How *desperately*, how *badly*, how *frantically* she had to pee.

The camera didn't show how Honey got a pan for her to pee in. All the camera showed was the pee gushing out of her pussy. People—men only, probably—watching would think that she just peed— that she didn't care if there was a pan under her or not.

She saw herself being raised again, so she was just on her toes—and she watched the man in the mask—the man the woman here called Werner— had whipped her again and again. She saw her own behind criss-crossed with red welts, one or two of them dripping blood. She knew that some would never disappear.

She watched herself collapse. Then Honey forced her to her knees and then snapped the dog leash into her labia ring and made her crawl out of camera range.

The video screen went black, momentarily, then:

WATCH FOR
THE SEQUEL TO
TATTOOED & TAMED
COMING SOON

The screen went black again. The video was turned off.

A sequel! Frank didn't tell her about any sequel. She looked at him searchingly. He appeared unconcerned. The women's fingers slid and down on Helen's slit.

"We have spoken to Frank—we'll distribute this video and have handled others like this. (Helen thought the women might have said distributed *many* others like this—)

"We are agreed. When you are ready—when your behind is fully recovered—" Helen was watching Frank, and trying to discern what he was thinking.

"Look at me—" The woman slapped Helen hard on her right breast. The slap stung. Helen turned to the woman on the sofa.

"When you have fully recovered, I think you'll

do just fine in a sequel. I think that a number of our *friends*—" Helen knew instinctively she meant *customers* "—will enjoy watching you in a sequel. What shall we plan? Shall we consider what you'd like to do or—what? Shall we surprise you? I think that would be best -" The woman was obviously taunting her.

"We'll also need an interview—to start the sequel—"

The interview—

The woman—who Frank knew only as Ms. Williams—told him what she wanted. For the interview she wanted a contrast between virginal white and the panther tattoo and the ring.

She told Frank to take "the little creature" and get a white garter belt, white stockings and white four-inch spike high heels.

They arranged a night and time to bring her back to the Nob Hill condo.

Frank brought her back to the condo—as arranged—using the old sedan he borrowed again from a biker's wife. They would not have been let into the underground parking garage on Frank's chopper, even with the OK of Ms. Williams.

They met at her condo—Helen was wearing

the last pair of designer jeans (again)—a t-shirt that said *The Roamin' Eye* on the top, a motorcycle in the middle and *Oakland* on the bottom.

Helen, Frank and the woman took a elevator up several floors—the woman opened the door of a different condo. It had only a sofa against one wall—empty. But Helen saw that a video camera was already on a tripod, two floodlights were on one side and two on the other, in a semi-circle. And another camera was on the floor, apparently a shoulder-held model. Otherwise the condo seemed empty.

The woman asked Helen to put on the garter belt, stockings and spike heels.

Helen did so, in corner of the room, turning her back to Frank and the woman.

She walked toward the two.

"Again," the woman said, "Now, please." Handcuffs, again.

Helen put her hands behind her back—the woman locked the handcuffs on her, then held out a chain—which she locked into Helen's ring. It was a medium weight chain that hung almost to her ankles.

"OK?" said Frank.

Now that Helen was handcuffed—he wasn't interested in just a video taped conversation.

Helen couldn't possibly escape from the woman, handcuffed and wearing spike heels.

"While we're waiting for the camera crew, I want to show you something."

She took from a corner a small chrome shaft, with a flared base, and an electric cord hanging from the base, then about six feet to a small control box, then another ten feet or so to a wall plug.

"This was made for us by an ingenious friend. What do you think it is?"

"A vibrator?"

"Almost. We had a little creature here recently. About your age and size, actually. She said she didn't want to do this—she didn't want to do that—she wouldn't do this or that or the other. My, what were we to do? About that one?" she said, in mock panic.

"I had a small paper clamp—the little black ones with two side flaps or prongs—you've seen them a million times. You pull the prongs together and the clamp opens and you can clamp perhaps 40 sheets of paper with that little office clamp.

"How can I put it—as your biker friends would say?—I clamped it carefully on one side of her little pussy—and this—" she held up the chrome rod— "would go easily into her little behind. Perfectly easily, because, as we discovered, she had let a lot of men use her there. So with a minimum of lubrication, we did insert it. She scarcely felt it.

"Now, I am sure, you have seen—in lightning storms—that lightning hits the highest—or closest—metal object. The top of the Empire State Building has been hit by lightning hundreds or perhaps thousands of times by now—"

Helen had no real idea where she was going with this story.

"With this inserted in her tender behind—and the clamp on her—on her pussy—she said *No* and then she said *No* again.

"The control box has a green light that shows the power is on, a dial showing low, medium, and high settings and a push button.

"When the button is pushed, in a split second an electrical current surges through her most sensitive areas and hits the nearest metal object. The clamp on her pussy.

"On the low setting, the little creature screamed and blacked out. On the middle setting, she would have been knocked unconscious. The highest setting would have permanently damaged her insides.

"The man who built this for us called it 'riding the lightning bolt.'

"After that, the little creature was willing, *yes I will, yes I will, yes I will,* to do anything *anything,* if that wasn't used again. All we had to do was mention 'riding the lightning bolt.'

"If you ever make a decision and I say something about 'riding the lightning bolt,' perhaps you would need to quickly reconsider what you just said or decided.

"The lightning bolt would surge through you directly to your ring."

The woman put that away and they waited for the camera crew.

Helen felt sick. She wondered what ever happened to that poor girl.

Helen stood about four feet in front of the camera. The woman turned down the room lights and turned on the floodlights. Helen couldn't see anything beyond the lights—

"Now," the woman, said, "standing in front of Helen—"I am going to ask you questions, from behind the lights. Your answers should be *very, very graphic*. You have no modesty here. None. Nothing. And of course, you will be very polite. Say 'yes ma'am' and 'no ma'am.'

"If the first thing I ask you is—'what are you?' your answer should be '*I'm a hot little whore*.'"

Helen remembered thinking, then saying once:

I'm not a whore—whores get paid for it—

She got as far as saying *I'm not a whore*—when the woman slapped her face. Hard. The chain danced near her ankles. She tottered and nearly fell, slipping on her spike heels. The woman had to catch her before she fell.

"That's exactly what you *will* say—that and everything else. The second thing you should say is '*I'm a bitch in heat*.'

"And everything else those bikers you know say at that bar."

Helen's face felt red and burning.

She remembered what she had once said to Frank:

Got any dark chocolate pussy nearby?

And when she was standing at the bar in the Roamin' Eye and a biker came up and said to Frank "getting any of that tonight?"

And she remembered what she said—

He gets it anyway he wants it. Any way. Any time. Almost any way he wants it. Almost any way—

"Oh," she said, more to herself than to the woman in front of her.

You want severe nasty—

The woman seemed surprised.

"Yes, exactly. *Severe nasty.* All the nasty things you can you say out of that nice soft mouth."

"They're here," the woman said. Helen assumed the camera crew.

Helen waited. Standing with her legs spread, clearly showing the ring and the padlock and the chain.

"Starting in a minute" the woman said, and a pause, then—

"You are here voluntarily?"

"Yes, ma'am."

"And what are your measurements?"

"Between a 34 and a 36. Maybe a 35. Between a B cup and a C cup—" She paused—"ma'am."

And then the question—

"And what are you?"

"I'm a hot little whore."

"And what else?"

"A bitch in heat—" pause. "Ma'am."

"And so—you visited a bar biker once out curiosity and met a biker and left the bar with him that night—and stayed with him weekends, then moved in with him—?"

"Yes, ma'am."

"And then what? He—well—he fucked you every day—or nearly every day and you sucked him every night—yes?"

Helen thought to try and tell her that she had been locked in Frank's loft and he had locked all her clothes away and kept her wearing nothing but panties, but she didn't know how to explain all that.

"Yes." Pause. "Ma'am."

"Did he wear out your little insides?"

"Yes, I'm always sore. Ma'am."

"Did you tell him that?"

"No—he'd only want to make it worse."

"Did he have a favorite position—all those days and days, every day getting your little self fucked?"

"He put me on my back and told me to put my legs up to my chest and point my feet at the ceiling. Then he put my ankles on his shoulders. That tipped my butt up toward him as if I was offering him my pussy. When he entered me, he dropped his full weight on me—I was trapped—curled up in a small ball under him. He always wanted to see how deep he could thrust in me. I couldn't move in that position—" pause. "Ma'am. Not at all.

"When he was in me like that I often had an odd image of - something—a flexible rod of some kind or—something other—with a cock head—entering my pussy—going all the way through me—and the cock head coming out my mouth. Completely impaling me—"

"And you sucked him every night?"

"Yes. It made my mouth and jaws sore too. I slept with his cock in my mouth all night. I seemed to always have the taste of his cum in my mouth."

"Did he ask for that?"

"He demanded it, Ma'am."

"And you had a session with a biker woman while he—and a biker friend—watched?"

"Yes. Ma'am."

"Had you ever kissed a woman before—a real girl-to-girl kiss?"

"No ma'am. "

"And—?"

"It was nice. She was soft and nice."

"Did you two care that two men were watching?"

"After a minute or so we didn't notice. Ma'am."

"I'm sure not," she said.

Helen was suddenly tired and stiff. And fully, completely, aware her hands were securely cuffed behind her back.

"Ma'am—may I move please—may I kneel? I'm very—"

Then she was aware of how somehow—somehow how erotic this was—to be controlled so completely by this woman. Not a man, but a woman—who had locked her into wrist cuffs—something totally erotic about this that she'd hadn't quite experienced before.

She felt herself getting wet again and shivering slightly.

"Stay where you are—after a while, perhaps. Don't move. Not now."

"Yes ma'am," Helen said. There was something *really erotic* about how she was completely *owned* by this woman.

"Ma'am," she tried again. "Your little bitch is in heat now—" she realized what she was saying, but said it anyhow.

"Your little bitch in heat—your little hot whore needs—"

The woman walked out into the floodlights. She was now wearing a short, almost mini-skirt length black skirt, thigh high boots and a leather corset-type top.

"Kneel. Right now. Little whore."

She helped Helen kneel, It was hard to do balancing on her high white spike heels and with her wrists cuffed behind her back.

The woman stood over her.

"Like pussy, little one?

"Are you a lesbian?

"A total little whore who does it all the time with men, but likes it better with girls?

"So tell me about your tongue in a little bare pussy—"

"I did like it—a soft completely shaved pussy is a cute part of a girl—"

The woman abruptly changed the subject.

"Keep thinking that of that pussy—but now—we haven't heard the rest of your story—I understand that your biker man wanted you to work in a topless place—"

"He took me to a topless place. I was supposed to be a topless dancer, but I bargained with the manager to be a waitress for the first two weeks. In a short mini-skirt costume that made me look like a tart. In high heels, hours a day. Every day some man slapped my butt or tried to reach under my miniskirt.

"After two weeks I told the manager I couldn't do it anymore.

"Then Frank was furious.

"I don't quite know what happened—I think I was drugged or something—when I woke up I had this ring deep in my—and the tattoos—and the small padlocks in my pierced ears—

"The ring has closed me so much that I have to squat to pee—and I have to be on a leash and he watches me pee. I guess all men would like to watch how a woman pees—"

"And—?"

"When I had a first period after I got this ring—I can't use a tampon—I can't possibly get one in me. I asked him to bring me some of those adult diapers. But he always *conveniently* forgot. So I had to hold a towel between my legs.

"He used my mouth then. He said my mouth was just as soft and wet as any pussy. Maybe better, he said.

"Ma'am—can I move some?—I really need to change position somehow."

"Stay right there whore. You're fine. Then what?"

"They took some pictures of me—in an empty motorcycle shop. With big motorcycles. Harley Davidsons. I was naked I think. High boots maybe. Not much else on. They took photos of me leaning on a motorcycle. Lying on top of the seat and gas tank. Kneeling beside the motorcycle. All afternoon. Pose this way—turn this way—all of the shots showed a chain padlocked to my ring.

"Every shot—and the other end of the chain padlocked to a motorcycle. Locked to the engine or handlebars. Or—or—she tried to remember all the positions.

"All of them clearly showed my ring, and a chain padlock to the ring. My legs spread. and the other end locked to a motorcycle.

"—The ultimate biker bitch-" she paused.

"And—the pictures—?"

Helen realized this woman knew every incident—maybe better than she could remember.

"I thought the pictures were to be private, ma'am—but—" she paused again.

" I agreed to be a bartender at the biker bar. I was to wear a short skirt, high boots—a biker t-shirt. No panties. A push-up bra or braless—"

"The first night I got to the bar—the pictures had been made into posters—maybe 4 feet by 6 feet, some of them. A picture of me kneeling in front of a red Harley Davidson. My ring clearly shown—and I was chained to the motorcycle—

"A close up of my ring and a chain padlocked to the ring.

"And others—big posters—every biker knew they were they. By the pool tables ands the pinball machines."

"And—bartending—?"

"I had a short pleated skirt,—it looked like a high school girl's cheerleader skirt. And I had a biker t-shirt on—

"Behind the bar there was a rung inset into the bar. I was told to stand still—behind the bar—and lift my skirt—A cable was padlocked to the ring in the bar and the other end padlocked into my ring. I could move maybe 5 feet to one side before there was no slack left in the cable. And five feet to the other side.

"All the bikers knew I was padlocked to the cable—ma'am."

"And what did you feel?"

"Humiliation. Constant humiliation. All the bikers—they all thought I was animal—or—worse—and the panther tattoo—"

"And there was an auction—?"

She knew everything.

"Sometimes they close the bar and auction off a woman for the night. A reverse auction. They start at $100 and work down. The lower the wi*nning*—"she emphasized it "—the winning price, the cheaper the woman feels.

"A biker woman bought me for all night for 69 cents—for all night—ma'am.

"She wanted me to—*ahhh*—do her—but I fell asleep. She wouldn't let me do her in the morning—she said I lost my chance—

"And then I was whipped—"

The woman told her to stand up, hold up one foot, then the other. She took off Helen's white spike heels, then Helen was told to get back on her knees, facing away from the cameras. The woman caressed her behind—and Helen was sure that the cameras were getting close-ups of the scars on her behind.

"Some of them won't ever disappear—" the

woman said. "You know that—and you may always have crop marks on your behind—" Before Helen could say anything—"They are quite exotic—"

She was told to turn around and stay on her knees. She turned, awkwardly.

The woman looked down.

"Your measurement, again—?"

"About a 35—not a 34 or a 36—between a B-cup and a C-cup—"

The woman stood behind her, Leaned over and cupped both breasts with her hands.

"You might like to have a bigger—*set*—perhaps—a lot of Hollywood girls get a new pair- -it's quite common—"

Helen didn't know what to say.

"I'm thinking of 46 D—"

"But—that would be grotesque—far too big for me—my—chest—is too small—"

"46 D—" the woman said again.

"*No—no—no,* " Helen repeated over and over.

The woman bent over and whispered into her ear.

"Don't move, little whore—not an inch."

Helen was on her knees, Her wrists still in handcuffs behind her back, her knees spread, the chain in a loose pile between her knees.

little whore, little whore, whore whore—she heard herself saying.

The bikers in the Roamin' Eye bar still called her Padlock, but she knew that would soon change. Soon it would be the *whore behind the bar with a ring in her pussy.*

And the woman here, just called her *little whore.* It made her feel, humiliated, warm—and wet.

Humiliated every time—but somehow—in a way she could not say to herself—somehow, *well—right.* And she did say, toward the video cameras behind the stage lights—"*I'm a hot little whore.*"

The woman walked a step or so toward her.

"Don't move, don't move a fraction of an inch."

The woman pushed her chin down with her right thumb and pushed her head down with her left hand.

"Keep your head down."

The woman took three steps toward the stage lights, speaking into the dark where she knew video cameras were running.

"She'll feel very heavy wit 46 D or 46 double D tits. Standing up she won't be able to see her own feet. And without holding something, she'll feel like she's falling forward if she walking wearing four inch spike heels.

"She'll have to learn how to walk all over again. And there will probably few clothes that will fit her top, and the rest of her chest."

She came over to Helen and whispered in her ear.

"Remember something about 'riding the lightning bolt'?"

She cupped each of Helen's breasts underneath and held them up—as if presenting them to the video cameras.

"46 D cups—soon—maybe 46 double D—"

She bent down and whispered to Helen again.

"I am going to lift my skirt. You kiss my panties right over my pussy. And say 'Thank you—'"

She stepped away, lifted her skirt and stepped toward Helen.

Helen kissed her black panties.

"Thank you," she said weakly.

The woman bent down again and whispered.

"Say it again and mean it. Little whore. And keep your mouth on my panties."

She stepped toward Helen again.

"Thank you ma'am," Helen said, a bit louder. She kissed the woman's black panties.

The woman held the back of her head again and kept Helen's mouth on her panties.

"On more time, little whore—"

She kept Helen's face tightly against her panties.

"*MMmmmm mmmmm—*"

The lights went out.

The videotaping was over.

Earlier—In the Condo—

"We'll also need an interview—to start the sequel—" the woman had said.

"Frank—" Helen pleaded. The man in the black slacks and black shirt came over and stood over her, blocking her view o Frank.

"Frank has sent us several other actresses to us—" (Helen new that *actresses* were girls like herself, paddled and whipped.)

"All of them have worked out very nicely. We would be disappointed in you, Padlock—if you were uncooperative—"

Helen looked up at this man.

"We have paid very good money for some actresses. Frank's methods are sometimes crude but effective. Then we—shall I say—put the finishing touches on his work. It is beneficial to us all—"

So that was what happened to Frank's previous girlfriend.

Somehow she joined these people.

The man suddenly changed the subject.

"You have been very nicely tattooed. That makes you valuable. Don't worry. You won't be mistreated. You'll just star in a film—now and then. That won't hardly be so bad, will it? Otherwise, women not so valuable learn that there are much harder ways to live. Day by day.

"Those who are trained—those who have been trained—who then become disobedient—learn in a how much their disobedience costs them."

Helen thought the man spoke in a very careful, contrived way. But she knew well what he was saying.

"We have paid a high price for you—" he continued.

"And we have contacts all over the world. There are many who could afford you and would earn us a fine profit, indeed, for you.

"People who collect women such as yourself. You have an advantage because you have been trained. Some one else won't have to start from scratch with you and that makes you very valuable. And your tattoo and ring makes you even more valuable—"

She had been sold!

Like she was a horse or a champion steer.—

Sold by Frank to thee people for god knows how much or for what purpose.

A sequel to that film—well that would only take a few hours—Then what? What would they do to her then? Or make her do?

Helen couldn't imagine what they would have in store for her. She knelt with her wrists cuffed behind her, wearing the same nightgown and camisole, garter belt and stockings that she had worn during the film. When she had been paddled then whipped. And her ring. Permanently deep inside her. They wouldn't forget that either.

She wanted to talk to Frank, to find out what he had sold her for—what she would be doing for these people—what Frank knew about them—how long he had known them—but the man in black was still standing in front if her, blocking her view of Frank.

"We know the man who did your art work—your tattoo," the man in front of her said.

"We may call on him again. Shall you have something above your pussy? On your back? We will think it over—"

The woman on the sofa stood up. Helen suddenly remembered that she was wearing the dog leash, attached to the ring in her labia.

"We have paid a high price for you, Padlock—" the woman said.

"Kneel in front of me with your knees spread, please." Helen was sitting on her heels, but awkwardly got up and knelt on the carpet, with her knees about a foot apart.

"Frank tells me that you slept all night—that he trained you to sleep all night in a special way—how was that?"

Helen looked up at her.

"I—" she hesitated, "he asked me—no, he made me - " she finally said it—they knew it all anyhow—

"I spent all night with his thing in my mouth. I sucked him all night. Night after night—"

She was suddenly humiliated but somehow

proud at the same time, of what she had been trained to do.

"And he told us that you loved being tethered to the bar. With the cable attached to the ring deep in your—" the woman hesitated ever so slightly.

"In your labia. That you get terribly excited when you are tethered—with the cable locked to your—pussy—is that right? The cable running up under your little shorty skirts, Yes? That you begged him to somehow rape you after you worked all night in the biker's bar tethered by the cable behind the bar. Isn't that right?"

It was right. She was right. Helen remembered how wet she had gotten when she was tethered to the bar by the cable. When all the bikers knew she had nothing on under her mini-skirt and that she was ringed and padlocked to the cable. She *had* been a bitch. All those years. But Frank had treated her exactly how she should be treated. She was no longer a bitch. She might as well tell these people.

"Yes ma'am," she suddenly said. "I do get so excited.—when I was chained. Padlocked to the cable in the bar. When all the men knew I didn't have anything on under my skirt when I was padlocked to the bar—"

The woman watched her.

"I hurt so badly during the film. When I was paddled and whipped so. You saw—I peed—I hurt so badly—I don't think my behind is so sore now. I'll heal—"

She didn't know what else to say.

"You enjoy you your ring?" The woman asked.

"Yes," Helen said. The woman knelt down and loosened Helen's nightgown.

"We'd like to see you naked now." The woman unlocked Helen's wrist cuffs.

Helen undressed for them. The dog leash was still snapped in her ring. She stood naked in front of them three of them, making not the slightest move to unsnap the leash. Frank and the couple in black. The woman held Helen's leash so there was some slack in it.

"I think you are terribly wet now, aren't you?"

Helen nodded. Then she thought—"does the new film start soon?"

"Yes," the woman said. " Very soon. I think you'll enjoy it—"

"Yes ma'am," Helen said.

"And what will you be—after the next film?"

"An obedient and well-trained whore," she said.

. . . to be continued. . . ?

www.ingramcontent.com/pod-product-compliance
Lightning Source LLC
Chambersburg PA
CBHW070826180626
46818CB00001B/414